The whole house was brightly illuminated by candles.

Maybe it hadn't been a power outage. Maybe they had cut the power for the ambiance.

As I reached the foyer, I froze.

It was her. It was the girl. Standing there next to the grandfather clock. She was looking in the other direction, but I had a clear view of her profile.

The same long dark hair that had haunted my dreams for fifteen years. The same luscious lips. The same smoky eyes.

But something was fundamentally wrong with this.

I was older, but she was not.

Good God.

Did schizophrenia run in my family?

TRAPPED IN THE MELODY

ALSO BY KATHRYN KALEIGH

THE BECQUERELS

Twist of Fate

When the Stars Align

Once in a Blue Moon

Once Upon a Christmas

A Wish Upon a Star

Written in the Wind

Scripted in the Stars

Destined in the Twilight

Promised in the Mist

Trapped in the Melody

When Lightning Strikes

Storm of Time

Midnight Storm

When the Moon Falls

Stormborn Angel

Time Tempest

The Heart Remembers

A Moment in Time

Moonlight Shadows

Rescued in Time

TRAPPED IN THE MELODY

THE BECQUERELS

INTO THE MIST

KATHRYN KALEIGH

TRAPPED IN THE MELODY

PREVIEW: SECOND CHANCE KISSES

Written by Kathryn Kaleigh

Published by KST Publishing, Inc., 2022

Cover by Skyhouse24Media

www.kathrynkaleigh.com

Created with Vellum

To learn more about Kathryn Kaleigh, visit

www.kathrynkaleigh.com

Kathryn Kaleigh

PROLOGUE

EMMA BECQUEREL

November 1855

My fingers slid easily over the smooth piano keys, the strains of what was supposed to be a joyful melody filling the evening air.

I winced as I hit a wrong note, throwing off the whole piece. As long as I looked at the music, I could play okay, but Mother insisted that I practice playing by memory.

Even now, mother sat across the room next to the warmth of the fireplace, working her needlepoint. I shivered. It hardly seemed fair. I, too, wanted to sit in front of the warm fire and read.

Shivering, even with a shawl draped around my shoulders, I wore a long-sleeved light blue wool dress with a full skirt that belled out around me when I stood up. Not like a ball gown, but a normal day dress.

I didn't particularly like playing the piano. Not really. I wouldn't mind being a pianist, but since I wasn't willing to put in the countless hours of practice, I would never get to that professional level where I could entertain guests with my skills.

So even though I knew it and Mother knew it, she would never admit that I was wasting my time playing every evening.

I would much prefer to work at my sketches or to sit and read. Either one would be far more enjoyable to me. I found much more meaning in those things than I did learning an instrument whose sole purpose was to impress and entertain others.

The grandfather clock standing in the foyer chimed the hour telling me I had only thirty minutes left to play before I could be excused.

The clock's chimes joined in with the piano's melody, softening the notes of the song I played.

Now that I was seventeen, old enough for a husband, I could be married soon and be out from beneath my mother's iron thumb.

Although I had been reluctant to accept the idea, I was beginning to think that maybe it was time.

My fingers still on the keys, I looked to my right, toward the shadowy foyer.

And that's when I saw him.

A tall, lean young man standing at the door watching me play. He wore a short dark coat and an odd-looking cap.

I missed a few notes, then just started playing the one song I knew from memory, so I wouldn't have to look back at the music.

A quick glance in Mother's direction told me she didn't notice the change in melody, nor did she see the man. She hadn't even looked up from her needlepoint.

Perhaps the man was one of Father's guests. It was odd, though, because the stranger appeared to be alone. No one was with him. Not Father. Not the butler.

I wondered if I should be alarmed, but he didn't look dangerous.

As my song ended, Mother looked up at me with that look that insisted I keep playing.

So I did and even though I kept my eyes on the sheet music, I had trouble keeping my place. It was most disconcerting with the stranger watching me like this.

I stole a glance toward him. He stood at the doorway, leaning against the doorframe, watching me. He was young. My age. And very handsome.

My fingers stumbled.

Unable to play any longer, I lifted my fingers from the keys. I closed my eyes and counted to ten.

"I'm sorry, Mother," I said. "I'm not feeling well. I have to stop."

Mother just shrugged.

"Very well," she said. "You can be excused."

I cautiously raised my gaze to the foyer, but the man was no longer there.

I hadn't seen him leave. I watched the foyer a moment, but he didn't come back.

Perhaps I had imagined him.

I straightened the piano music and put it away, tucking it beneath the bench seat for tomorrow when it would be there to torture me again.

I headed out of the parlor before Mother changed her mind.

As I crossed through the doorway into the foyer, I could smell the man who had just been standing there.

A deep woodsy scent with undertones of lavender.

It woke all my feminine sensibilities.

Yes. It was time for me to think about taking a husband.

1

JAMES BOUCHERON

Present Day

To say that I was down on my luck was an understatement.

Stabbing the shovel deep into the soft earth, I dug up a dried out dead plant, roots and all, and tossed it into the wheelbarrow.

I had to stop and pull off my flannel shirt, tossing it aside. Between the warmth of the morning sun and the warmth radiating from the pile of leaves and debris behind me, I was no longer cold.

I dumped my collection of debris from the wheelbarrow onto the fire and used a rake to keep the flames from spreading. Little sparks flew high into the sky, hopefully cooling off before they landed in one of the huge oak trees overhead. The leaves were falling off the limbs, but the moss didn't appear to be affected by the cold November weather.

The house behind me was a large four-story Greek style

house with large white columns lining the veranda. The wooden columns, painted white, had withstood the centuries surprisingly well. But the house, built in the early 1800s, badly needed a coat of paint. Maybe I would get to that next.

I'd been to the Becquerel Estate once before when I was a teen. My father had come here on business with Jonathan Becquerel and I'd come with him.

We'd only been here for one night, but the place had left a lasting impression on me.

Other than that, I couldn't explain why I had been drawn to this place when I lost everything.

We had been wealthy. Billionaires. But for two years, one wrong turn after another had steadily pulled us down. Then my father's death had put a nail in not only his coffin, but that of any wealth the family had as well.

I had left Atlanta as a debtor.

Though I had not thought it was possible, I found myself literally on the streets with nothing but the clothes on my back.

One night in the homeless shelter had been one night too many.

I'd left the next morning, hitchhiking my way to Natchez. It had taken me three days.

From there, I had set off walking toward the Becquerel Estate. Between walking and riding on the back of someone's pickup truck, I'd made it here from town in two hours.

Jonathan Becquerel, the owner of this old place, was older now, moving slowly, and had a caregiver named Tracie who lived with him.

Tracie hadn't liked it when Jonathan had taken me in and after a long conversation he'd agreed to give me a place to stay in exchange for helping him out around here.

God knows he needed the help.

Tracie stayed busy inside, doing a decent job of keeping things up, though most of her time was spent caring for

Jonathan. Needless to say, the outside of the house had been neglected.

I wasn't a gardener, by any means, but I was good with my hands and I was a quick learner.

My parents had given us chores—indoor and outdoor—when we were growing up, so I was somewhat acquainted with manual labor. Fortunately Jonathan had gloves I could wear.

This mindless work gave me time to think.

I needed to come up with a plan.

My father may have left me penniless, but I had skills. I had a master's degree in finance and had worked for my father. I knew the markets.

The problem was, however, that I was flat out broke.

I would come up with a way out of this mess.

I didn't know what the solution was yet, but I'd come up with something.

My gaze was drawn toward the house again.

I'd never forgotten what I had seen that night I'd stayed here with my father.

The vision of the most beautiful girl I'd ever seen sitting at the piano had haunted me over the last fifteen years. She'd had long blonde hair framing a heart shape face. Large dark eyes and lush lips curled into a sexy little pout.

I could still see her clearly. I could hear the badly played music.

The odd thing was that neither Jonathan nor my father had seen her nor had they heard the music.

And they had been standing right next to me.

2

EMMA

November 1858

Three years had passed since that night I'd seen the man standing in the foyer.

And for three years he'd haunted my dreams.

And despite my decision—one I had made that very night—to choose a husband, I'd compared every eligible bachelor who came within my path to him.

A man I had not even met. I had not seen him up close. I didn't know his name. No one else had even seen him.

Apparently, Father had not had any guest that night.

So even though I believed I had invented the man—I even referred to him as "The Man" in my thoughts—he was the one I compared all others to.

"Where is your dance card?" Mother asked as we walked together toward the stairs.

It was the annual Becquerel Autumn Ball and everyone who was anyone would be in attendance. That meant there would be countless eligible bachelors in need of a wife. Whether or not they knew they needed a wife was another matter entirely.

"It's right here," I said, lifting the dreaded dance card strapped to my wrist. After countless balls and barbeques, I knew that there would be no one here who matched the image I carried in my head.

Already the music from the orchestra drifted upstairs and people were making their way in through the front door.

The French doors would be open to allow cool air inside and to allow guests to spill outside, provided the weather didn't get too cold.

Carriages were lined up along the oak tree canopied lane, each family eagerly waiting their turn to come inside and join the festivities.

Everyone knew that my brother, Martin, was home from West Point, so whether Mother wanted to admit it or not, he was the main attraction at tonight's ball.

I didn't mind. It actually should have taken some of the pressure off me and it would have except that Mother wore her sternest expression as we made our way downstairs.

"Make sure you fill every dance," she said.

"Of course, Mother," I said, sighing to myself.

It was going to be a long night.

Unless there was someone new at tonight's ball… a marriageable gentleman I had yet to meet, I would be beleaguered by the same men I'd been dancing with for the past two to three years.

Handsy. Dull. Self-absorbed.

I had honestly grown somewhat disheartened that the handsome mystery man would show up again provided, of course, that I had not invented him in my own head.

Perhaps tonight things would change.

Fortunately, other than Mother, most people would be focused on my brother and not me.

Perhaps I'd be able to slip off to the library and avoid dancing with the most wearisome suitors.

As we neared the first floor, the clock began to chime.

Six chimes.

And off we went.

3

JAMES

The best thing about working for Jonathan Becquerel was that he allowed me to freely roam his home.

Although I didn't really know how he could possibly remember me, I hoped for his sake that he did.

Letting a total stranger into his home was dangerous and Tracie had every right to be cautious.

Three days had passed and still, she looked at me with suspicion whenever our paths crossed. Smart girl.

Except in this case, I'd been honest and I was harmless.

At any rate, the best part of being here, besides having a safe, comfortable place to stay, was having access to his computer and Internet. Since I didn't have so much as a cell phone at the moment, I would have otherwise been completely out of touch with the world.

I watched YouTube videos and took countless notes, hoping for some inspiration as to how to essentially start over.

Alone.

My father had done it. His parents had brought him here from France and he had started with nothing.

I could do it, too.

But Father had taken us down hard.

And that was going to be even harder to come back from.

My name, for those who recognized it, was tainted with failure.

I considered changing my name and held that in reserve for a last resort.

We were still a good family. My father's financial failures shouldn't change that.

Shouldn't was always a key word.

I barely noticed when the rain started, coming down outside the window behind me, but when lightning struck near me, I was reminded that I was in the country.

I was even more reminded ten minutes later when the electricity went out.

I'd moved over to the armchair, bringing the laptop computer with me.

The only light in the room came from that computer.

The Internet was fried. No service.

That must have been some lightning strike. My ears were ringing and I couldn't hear a thing.

I slowly closed the lid and set the computer on the table next to me.

Had there been a table there earlier? I couldn't remember.

I stood up, then I heard the music.

Not music from a television or a radio.

Not piano music like I'd heard that night fifteen years ago.

But orchestra music. And live orchestra music if I remembered anything from life before.

I crossed to the door and stopped.

There was a party on the other side of that door. I'd stake my life on it.

And considering that my life was really all I had left, that was saying something.

I opened the door and poked my head out.

A tall, debonair, and distinguished man walked in my direction. He carried himself as a butler would.

"Good evening," he said, stopping two feet in front of me. "Can I be of assistance?"

"I'm a little confused," I said.

"My name is Villars. I'm the butler." His gaze swept over me, almost imperceptibly.

"I need to see Jonathan," I said.

"Jonathan," the man said. "Right." Then he leaned forward. "Might I make a suggestion?"

"Of course," I said. The man reminded me of the butler I'd grown up with. His name had been Edgar and he'd always been present in our household the whole time I'd lived at home.

Sadly enough, I didn't even know what had become of Edgar.

"If you'll wait here," he said. "I'll bring you something appropriate to wear."

I smiled. And just like Edgar, Villars was here to look out for us.

4

EMMA

Not having been able to escape her yet, I stood in the foyer with Mother.

As she waited for the next family to come inside, we stood with Doc and Mrs. White. It was the first time I'd seen them here in quite some time. Something had happened, a rift in the family perhaps, but I wasn't privy to what it was.

At the moment, Doc White had a sling around his shoulder and was leaning on a cane. He'd been thrown by a horse last week on his way to see a patient.

"Emma plays the piano quite well," Mother told them. "Don't you Emma?"

"I dabble a bit," I said, modestly, silently pleading with Mother not to embarrass me by making me play in front of all these people.

Heavens.

Mother knew I didn't play that well. She would not do that.

"Perhaps we can hear you play one day," Mrs. White said, kindly.

I nodded politely.

"Of course," Mother said. "We'll have to have you over some time. Just the two of you."

"Our son should be arriving shortly," Mrs. White said. "He's a doctor, too." She gestured toward her husband's arm. "He's been taking up all the slack since my husband's accident."

"That must be hard," Mother said.

Mrs. White turned to me. "Have you met my son, Edward?"

"No," I said. "I don't think so."

I was actually certain of it. I had a good memory for these things.

I also had a sinking feeling about meeting the young Doctor Edward White.

I had made the observation that anytime parents were eager to introduce their sons to a young lady, it was because they despaired of that son being capable of finding a wife on his own.

It was, of course, just my observation. Edward might be a fine young man.

Mrs. White leaned forward. "Save a spot for him on your dance card."

"Of course."

I glanced over Mother. She was actually smiling. That concerned me more than anything.

Unable to process that right now and since my little dance card hung from my left wrist, I decided to do it right now.

The first dance was about to start any minute and Edward was not here.

A perfect combination.

Using the little table in the foyer as a writing surface, I wrote Edward's name in the dance number one spot. Then for good measure, I also wrote his name in on dances number two and three.

There.

Assuming he was as late as I expected, I would not have to dance with anyone for at least the first three dances.

I turned back to the little group.

Mrs. White squeezed my wrist and smiled at me.

"It's was a pleasure seeing you again," Mother said, dismissing the couple. "Please. Enjoy yourself."

As Mother turned to greet the next family coming across the veranda, I took the opportunity to slip off, murmuring some excuse about being thirsty.

The truth was, it was early in the night and I'd already met my tolerance level for being sociable.

How was I ever supposed to marry and be a good hostess like my mother when I could barely make it through the first hour of introductions?

True to my word, I went to the punch table and took the cup someone handed me.

I took it with me and went to stand near the grandfather clock so I could watch everyone and see everything that was going on without being in the middle of it.

I saw Villars, the butler dash upstairs. Father probably needed something. A handkerchief perhaps.

But then Villars came back just a few minutes later with his arms full of what looked like men's clothing.

This was most certainly different.

If my wayward cousins, always into something, had been here, I wouldn't have been the least bit surprised by any such thing, but they were all married and living on their own.

I doubted any of them would come to the ball tonight, since they all had infants. If they did, I would be quite surprised.

I watched as Villars turned down the hall toward the dining room and I was just about to follow him when I was stopped.

"Miss Emma."

I immediately recognized Ben's voice.

Ben was one of the young men who always liked to get in a dance on my dance card.

And although we usually had a dance and a conversation together, we never moved beyond anything other than pleasant friendship. He never once asked to call on me. And I wasn't bothered by it.

Sometimes a girl just had a feeling about these things. And I had a feeling that Ben and I were destined to just be friends.

"Hello Ben," I said. "How are you?"

"Good," he said, grinning. "I just saw you talking with the Whites. Have you met their son?"

"No," I said, hiding the wrist with my dance card behind my back. I didn't want to have to explain how the mysterious Edward occupied a full one third of my dance card.

"I heard he's going to be here. I think you'll like him."

"So I've heard," I said with a little smile. If this Edward White was such a good catch, it seemed as though I would have heard of him by now.

After all, over the last three years, Mother had made sure I met all the eligible bachelors in the area.

Maybe he was a widower, I mused. Whatever the situation was, I was sure to find out soon enough.

"He's only just returned from medical school," Ben said. "That's why you haven't met him."

"Ah. I see." That actually made perfect sense.

"Did you save room on your dance card for me?" Ben asked, drawing my attention back to him.

"Of course," I said. "Are you available for the fourth dance?"

"I'm all yours," he said, with a quick bow. "See you then."

I wondered how the men kept their dances straight, since they didn't carry dance cards.

As he went about his way, blending in with the crowd, I went back to studying the mystery of why Villars would be bringing men's clothes downstairs in the middle of a ball.

5

JAMES

Villars guarded the door as I got dressed. He'd also brought a candle that chased away some of the darkness in the room.

"What soiree is this?" I asked.

"It's the annual Becquerel Autumn Ball," Villars said, proudly, straightening to his full height.

"Ah," I said, putting my arms in the cotton shirt and beginning to work on the small buttons. The shirt was obviously of good quality and was tailor made for someone. It was a little tight around the chest, but I could wear it without too much problem.

"Whose shirt is this?" I asked, mostly to make polite conversation.

"No one in particular," he said. "We keep extra clothes for… guests."

"I see," I said. Something wasn't adding up. Jonathan had failed to tell me something.

I shrugged it off as I fastened the cuffs. It was hard to complain about having the opportunity to wear nice formal clothes again.

"There's no generator?" I asked.

Villars looked at me as though I'd asked for a ride to the moon.

No answer.

I fastened the belt around my waist and shrugged it off.

Any butler worth his salt wouldn't gossip, nor would he provide too much explanation about things that weren't within his area of expertise.

"A handkerchief, Sir," Villars said, handing me a square white cloth.

"Thank you," I said, tucking the handkerchief in my pocket since I didn't know what else to do with it.

"Shall I introduce you?" Villars asked as I slipped on and tied the shoes he'd loaned me.

"What? No," I said. Then looked straight at Villars. "Actually… that's why I need to see Jonathan. I don't think I'm supposed to be here."

"Yes Sir," Villars said. "Jonathan isn't here."

"Oh." I stood up and pulled on the jacket. "Anything I should be concerned about?"

I didn't want to get into Jonathan's business. A man was entitled to his privacy, but Jonathan was getting up in age. If he'd taken ill and had to be hospitalized, I thought I should know.

"I don't think so." Villars tilted his head to the side.

I straightened the jacket. It fit surprisingly well. It was a rather interesting fashion, but this was the rural south, so I shrugged that off, too. I was not in a position to be choosy.

Villars held the door as I stepped through.

The clock began to chime the hour. I distinctly remembered *not* hearing the clock until now. Perhaps they only wound it for parties.

I was still concerned about Jonathan, but my concerns quickly shifted to trying to figure out the situation.

And what a situation it was.

The men were all dressed much like I was, but now that I was among them, I could see that the clothes were old-fashioned. 1800s. And even more conspicuous was that the women all wore long full dresses in bright colors.

I rubbed my chin as I considered.

Mardi Gras?

This part of the country was known for celebrating the flamboyant festival, but this was the wrong time of year for it. I'd gone to Mardi Gras once with some friends in college. It had been more than enough for me. Not my thing.

This could be anything. Villars had said it was an annual Autumn ball. Costumed but not masked. It would have been interesting to add masks.

But the music was good and the whole house was brightly illuminated by candles.

Maybe it hadn't been a power outage. Maybe they had cut the power for the ambiance.

As I reached the foyer, I froze.

It was her. It was the girl. Standing there next to the grandfather clock. She was looking in the other direction, but I had a clear view of her profile.

The same long dark hair that had haunted my dreams for fifteen years. The same luscious lips. The same smoky eyes.

But something was fundamentally wrong with this.

I was older, but she was not.

Good God.

Did schizophrenia run in my family?

6

EMMA

I felt him looking at me before I turned.

The heat crept up my cheeks and I fisted my hands in my skirts.

The echo of the clock's chimes hung in the air, floating beneath the orchestra music.

Slowly lifting my head and turning, I waited while Mrs. James and her daughter passed in front of me, deep in conversation, not even seeing me.

Then I saw him watching me.

I bowed my head in acknowledgement of his attention, then turned away, lifting my skirts just enough to avoid stepping on the hem.

But he reached my side and blocked my path before I had barely taken two steps.

"It's you," he said.

Lifting my chin, I looked him straight in the eyes. I had to look up because he was at least a head taller than me.

His eyes were startlingly blue. So blue I couldn't look away. Or maybe it was the way he was looking at me. I don't think anyone had ever looked at me quite this way before.

I quickly decided there was only one explanation. He was the young Doctor Edward White.

I decided this first of all because I hadn't seen this man before and second simply because he knew me. His parents must have pointed me out.

"Yes," I said. My voice felt surprisingly calm considering that I was trembling on the inside.

Neither one of us moved. I counted the seconds off along with the clock behind me.

After ten seconds, I held up my wrist.

"You're on my dance card," I said.

"Oh," he said, looking over my shoulder at the dancers already engaged in the first waltz. "That could be a problem."

"How so?" I tried to ignore the disappointment that washed through me.

In spite of my previous misgivings, I found myself quite attracted to this mysterious Doctor Edward White.

"I don't know how to dance…" he said, looking back at me. "like that."

"That's okay," I smiled. "We can go outside. Sit on the veranda instead."

"Are you sure?" he asked.

"It's quite alright," I said, needing to do something. I turned, lifted my skirts, and headed out the front door.

He followed at my heels.

Since there was a couple standing off to the right of the veranda, I led him toward the left. The only place for us to sit was on the swing.

The evening breeze was rather cool coming from across the river. The moon was full and bright, spilling across the front lawn, decorated with lanterns to light the path for the carriages.

"Is this okay?" I asked, glancing over my shoulder as I reached the white swing hanging by ropes from the ceiling.

"Perfect," he said, coming around to hold the swing steady while I sat down.

I rubbed my arms to chase away some of the unexpected evening chill.

"Cold?" he asked.

"A little," I said, "but the fresh air is nice."

He shrugged out of his jacket and carefully placed it over my shoulders.

"Better?" he asked.

"Yes. Thank you."

He sat down beside me, his weight noticeably shifting the swing.

"It's a beautiful night," he said.

I nodded, lost in my thoughts.

Oddly enough, I think I had just found the first man I'd ever wanted to court.

Maybe he reminded me of that man I'd seen standing in the foyer three years ago.

What if he was the same man?

But… that man had been my age.

7

JAMES

I was crossed between disbelief at my good fortune and concern for my own mental health.

Fifteen years ago I had seen a beautiful young lady sitting at the piano. In this very house.

This girl sitting on the swing next to me was the very same girl. I was certain of it. I had her features etched into my brain long, long ago.

She wasn't always the first thing I thought about when I woke up in the morning and wasn't always the last thing I thought about before I went to sleep, but over the years, I'd thought about her often. Sometimes even when I was dating someone, I'd find myself thinking about the mysterious girl. Wondering if I'd ever see her again.

Considering that I had been the only one to see her that day… to hear her music… had been odd.

Fortunately my father had been preoccupied. Otherwise I might have ended up with a psychological evaluation and who knows what my direction my life might have taken.

Although to be quite honest, I wasn't sure it could be much

worse than it was right now. I just might have gotten here sooner.

I had nothing. No home. No car. Not even a cell phone.

I was relying upon a man I hadn't seen for fifteen years… leaning on a business associate of my father's that I really didn't even know.

Not exactly the way a man would choose to play his life's hand.

Going from being a billionaire to a homeless man was not something I was proud of.

Fortunately, it didn't look like this young lady was currently asking questions.

"You must be having a hard time right now," she said. "With what happened with your father and all."

"What do you mean?" How could she possibly know about me and what I was going through. Had Jonathan told her?

"Well," she said, with a little smile. "It appears your father has left you in something of a bind."

She may not be asking questions, but she knew entirely too much for my comfort.

"I suppose you could say that, yes." I hadn't told Jonathan much, but I'd never expected him to tell everyone what little I did share. It was possible she had gotten this from another source.

"I'll be okay," I said. "I have plans for a fresh start."

"Oh," she said. "That's admirable."

I'd had enough of talking about me. Besides, I wanted to know about her. I wanted to know everything about her.

And after I learned everything about her, I wanted to know how she didn't appear to have aged.

"Tell me about you," I said. "I know nothing about you."

"Surely you know something," she said, tucking a strand of hair behind her ear.

I shook my head. "I don't even know your name."

She looked surprised. Quite surprised actually.

"It's Emma," she said. "My name is Emma Becquerel."

"Becquerel. How are you related to Jonathan?"

"I don't know him." She was looking at me a bit cautiously now.

"This is his house," I said with a wave of my arm. "Jonathan Becquerel."

She was shaking her head.

"I think you must be very confused, Edward. This is my home. I live here with my parents."

8

EMMA

I pulled Edward's jacket close around me and turned so that I could see him better.

I was beginning to think that this man that I found so handsome was actually quite uninformed.

I actually was beginning to think that he thought I was someone else.

But someone had pointed him in my direction. Hadn't they?

I had assumed it was his mother. But maybe he had found me on his own.

I should be grateful for that since I didn't trust mothers who pushed their sons at me.

Maybe he was just overworked. I suppose that could do that to a man.

But right now, while my thoughts were running rampant, he was looking at me as though I had gone insane.

"My name isn't Edward," he said.

"Oh. I'm so sorry." Whatever had possessed me to be so familiar with a strange man? "I meant Dr. White, of course. Please forgive me."

He was shaking his head.

"Dr. White?"

I looked toward the door. "The elder Dr. White… Actually Mrs. White, your mother, said you would be coming later."

I lifted my wrist to show him my dance card dangling by a ribbon.

"She told me to save a dance for you. But since you were late," I said, lowering my voice. "I rather took advantage and filled three spots with your name."

The man looked blankly at me a moment. Then he laughed.

He was so very handsome when he laughed. Even more handsome than before.

"Are you saying you didn't want to dance?" he asked.

I sat back, looking straight ahead now. Forcing my heart rate to go back to a manageable rate.

"I don't mind the dancing," I said, wrinkling my nose. "I just don't care for the men who would claim those dances."

"Yet you were willing to dance with me," he said.

I looked over at him sideways. "I suppose I was hopeful that you wouldn't be like them."

He settled back, making himself comfortable, adjusting the cuffs on his sleeves.

"Tell me what it is you don't like about them."

"That's easy," I said. "They're handsy, dull, and self-absorbed."

"I can see why you filled your dance card with someone you thought wasn't here." He grinned.

"At least you understand," I said. "My mother insists that I should be married by now."

"Why would she think that?" he asked. "you're quite young."

I felt him looking at me. Almost as though he were trying to figure something out.

He'd seemed to know me, yet obviously he did not.

He also thought that this house belonged to someone named Jonathan Becquerel.

I had lived here my whole life. I'd seen cousins come and go. But never once had I even met anyone named Jonathan Becquerel, much less had he lived here.

I also knew my family's history and there was no one by that name.

A logical woman would have gone inside, since something was obviously amiss with this man. I, however, needed to figure out what that was before I drew any further conclusions about him.

9

JAMES

I gently rocked the swing with both feet on the ground. The full moon spilled over the lawn as lightning bugs flashed as they left the safety of the grass. The scent of honeysuckle mixed with magnolias enveloped us.

A steamboat blew its mournful horn in the distance. Probably a tourist boat out for an evening dinner cruise.

Whatever charade this was, this young lady played it well.

Either that or my mind was much more inventive than I had ever given it credit for.

"Why did you say *it's you* when you first saw me?" she asked.

"You reminded me of someone I saw a long time ago."

She seemed to consider that as I continued to rock the swing back and forth.

"Someone you knew well?" she asked.

"No," I said. I had always been an honest man and I wasn't going to start lying now. If I'd been prone to lie about things, I would probably still have my family's fortune or at least enough of it to live a decent life. Not starting over by working in an old man's garden.

"I only saw her one time," I said. "and it was here. But now that I think about it, it couldn't possibly have been you."

I suppose it could have been this woman's mother.

I found that thought entirely unsettling.

That I would be old enough to be this woman's father made me nearly ill.

"Can I ask you something personal?"

"I suppose you can ask," she said, biting her lip and looked up at me from beneath her lashes in a decidedly flirty move. This was definitely not helping.

"How old are you?"

"I'm twenty-one," she said, without hesitation.

"Thank God," I murmured to myself. Even if I had seen this girl's mother at the piano that day, there was no way that this girl was young enough to be my daughter.

"I suppose you think I should be married by now, as well," she said, twirling a lock of hair around her finger.

"No," I said, regaining my composure. "Not at all. I think you're quite young. Too young to be married, actually."

She was looking at me those green eyes, her brow furrowed.

"And how old are you Dr. White?" she asked.

"That's a fair question," I said. "But I'm not Dr. White."

"Oh." Her eyes widened as she studied me.

"If you aren't Dr. Edward White," she asked. "then who are you?"

"My name is James Boucheron," I said.

She looked away again as though trying to decide how to proceed with this new information. I halfway expected her to leave me here and go back inside.

If she had heard of me, then she would know just how bad off I was. And no young lady in her right mind would want to be associated with a man who didn't have so much as a cell phone to his name.

But she didn't.

"It's a pleasure to meet you Mr. Boucheron," she said, seemingly forgetting her question about my age.

"Please call me James," I said. "Mr. Boucheron was my father."

"I understand," she said, with a little nod. "Where do you live?"

I wasn't sure how to answer that question.

I had lived in Atlanta. But now… now I lived here… with Jonathan at the moment.

Somehow my instincts told me this was not the time to tell her that.

"I live nearby," I said. It wasn't a lie. Not really. And I would explain it to her later.

10

EMMA

It seemed like such an intimate thing. Sitting here with James's jacket wrapped around me just as his gaze wrapped around me, making me feel like I was not only the most beautiful girl here, but the only girl here.

Yet I knew practically nothing about the man sitting next to me on the swing. I knew his name… now But that was it.

Bullfrogs joined in with the crickets to provide background music as the orchestra suddenly quieted for one of their breaks.

I only knew his name…

Except that he carried a deep woodsy scent… with… undertones of lavender.

I had a flashback to that evening when I had been playing the piano. That had been three years ago, but I had never seen the man again.

Although this man reminded me of him, this couldn't be him. This man was too old. At least ten years too old.

I studied his profile.

Was it possible it was the same man? I hadn't seen him up close. He had the same lean figure. So that was the same.

But since that man had been wearing a hat of some kind, I hadn't seen his hair. This man had thick dark hair. And a five o'clock shadow that gave him an edgy look.

It was his eyes that had me spellbound. They were startlingly blue as he turned and looked at me with that little smile that had my heart rate tripping up dangerously.

Now that the music had stopped, people began spilling out across the veranda.

"Do you want to get out of here?" he asked.

"Where to?"

He looked around a moment.

"There," he said. "We can go out to that gazebo."

It was a scandalous thing to do, but I found that I wanted to be alone with him. Sitting on the veranda with him was one thing, but going out to the gazebo, in the shadows, was another thing entirely.

But I didn't want Mother to try and pull me away to dance with some foolish man whose company I didn't like.

And if we stayed here, other women would be vying for his name on their dance card. Already, I'd seen a couple of appreciative glances shot in his direction. Then they had looked at me and turned away.

My presence could only deter them so long.

I knew these girls. They would be after a handsome man like James in no time. He was new blood.

"Okay," I said, feeling positively reckless.

He quickly stood up and held out a hand for me. As I put my gloved hand in his, his fingers wrapped around mine, and I smiled.

Like a couple of lovers in a tryst, we dashed off toward the gazebo.

The chilly night wind pulled a strand of hair loose from my headband. I would have tucked it back except that I needed my free hand to keep from tripping over my skirt.

By the time we reached the gazebo, I was winded.

James, however, seemed to be in fine shape, breathing as easily as if he had just walked across the room.

11

JAMES

Emma's cheeks were flushed by the time we reached the gazebo and her breath came in short gasps.

"How was this so…" she took a breath." Easy for you?" she asked, between trying to catch her breath.

"I go to the g—" I cut myself off, because I had gone to the gym in my previous life. I didn't any more. But I could go for a run any time. Running didn't cost anything.

I just smiled and swept a stray lock of hair out of her face and tucked it behind one of her ears.

Her features were so delicate. Her lips parted slightly.

There was something about her that had me enamored.

She hugged the jacket close around her shoulders, then looked at me with her brow creased.

"I saw Villars bringing some clothes downstairs earlier." She ran a hand over the sleeve of my jacket draped over her shoulders. "Were they for you?"

She was smart, this one.

"Yes," I said.

"Why? Why did you come to the ball without proper clothing?"

"I had a… mishap. I actually hadn't planned on being here for the ball tonight."

"But…" She appeared to struggle with her question. "You were invited? You know my family?"

"Sort of," I said. "I know Jo—"

"Jonathan Becquerel, I know."

"Yes." I leaned forward, my shoulder touching hers. "I'm a little worried about him."

"I'm a little worried about you," she said.

"Why is that?" I asked, unable to keep myself from smiling.

"Just everything." She shifted slightly so that our shoulders were no longer touching. "You claim to know someone who doesn't live here. Your lack of clothes."

The orchestra music started back up and people began going back inside.

I stared at the front door, my thoughts going in fifty different directions.

Maybe Emma didn't know Jonathan.

I tried to think about what this could be.

Jonathan may have failed to tell me everything.

This could be a fund raiser.

Perhaps this was some kind of role play.

Just because she said her name was Emma Becquerel did not mean it really was.

Frankly, it didn't matter to me. When this party was over, she could tell me who she really was.

I held out a hand for hers.

She looked at me questioningly, then put her hand in mine.

She wasn't the only one who could role play.

Something my father had said to me on several occasions came back to me.

Go big or go home.

I lightly kissed the back of her gloved fingers.

But this wasn't going to do.

I ran my hands up past her elbows, slipped my fingers beneath the edge of her glove and slowly peeled it down, baring her hand.

She looked at me with wide eyes as I took her bare hand in mine and kissed her palm.

I realized in that moment that whoever Emma was, she was not pretending.

This girl truly was an innocent.

12

EMMA

The others guests had all gone back inside. The unexpectedly cool air driving them back inside to the warmth of the fireplace.

I shivered.

Though not for the cold.

James was nothing if not forward.

He removed my glove and pressed his lips against my palm.

His lips were soft against my skin.

Soft and firm.

He had no hesitation about him.

But instead of pulling away from him, as a proper young lady would do, I wanted to get closer to him.

My response was scandalous and one I hadn't had before. Not to any of the other men who had attempted to court me.

I couldn't say what it was about this man that drew me to him.

Perhaps it was the way he smelled. That familiar scent. That deep woodsy scent with undertones of lavender. The one that had haunted me for three years.

The one that led me to decide that I did indeed need to take a husband, yet none of the men I had encountered met my standards.

Holding my bare hand in his, he cupped my cheek with his other hand.

He leaned close, his breath touching my skin. I put a palm against his hard chest.

I leaned forward, wanting more of his touch and my eyes drifted closed.

Then his lips were on mine. Gentle. Soft. Yet overwhelming.

I sighed, feeling like I had come to a place I'd been searching for my entire life.

He drew me against him, holding me close, letting my cheek rest against his chest.

Even though I hadn't known I needed to, I felt safe with him.

"Emma," he whispered.

"Yes?"

"I have to go."

"Why?" I asked, leaning back a bit so I could look into his blue eyes.

"I'm not supposed to be here."

"But—"

He put a finger lightly against my lips.

"I have some things I have to figure out before I can be here," he said. "with you."

"I don't understand." I had trouble getting the words past the lump in my throat.

"I don't either," he said. "but I just know."

Yet he wasn't moving.

"You have to go?" I asked.

"Yes." But he kept his hands linked with mine as though he was reluctant to let me go.

"Will you come back?" I asked.

"I'm not sure."

I nodded. I didn't understand. But I had a feeling that maybe I would. Later.

"Walk me home," he said, standing up and pulling me with him.

He took two steps and stopped, then pulled me into his arms.

I wrapped my arms around his waist and felt my heart breaking.

I'd only just found him and now he was going away.

It was like I'd found love in one breath and lost it in the next.

13

JAMES

Emma and I walked back to the house, hand in hand.

A cool north wind blew around us, scattering dry colored leaves through the air like oversized raindrops.

The happy music drifting from the house almost seemed to mock what I was feeling inside.

The scent of Emma's hair, magnolia and maybe daffodils, lingered on my shirt.

I didn't want to let her go, but I knew that I had to.

I had nothing to offer her.

Bottom line. I was a homeless man from Atlanta.

And this, I had concluded, was a fundraiser of some sort. I didn't know where Jonathan was, but I understood why he hadn't invited me. I had nothing to offer. Actually, it was quite possible that he had loaned or rented his home for the evening and it had slipped his mind to tell me about it.

To be at a fundraiser like this, Emma had to be from a wealthy family. And there were certain expectations that came with seeing a girl like this.

I couldn't date her without a car. A phone. All the trappings that came with success. All the things that were expected of a man worthy of her attention.

Once inside, I squeezed her hand and let her go.

"Go," I said, briefly touching her dance card. "Enjoy."

She looked at me with wide eyes full of moisture and I knew that she was feeling the same thing I was feeling.

She was no more going to enjoy the rest of this party than I was.

I kissed the back of her hand one more time, then turned and walked back toward the library.

As I passed the grandfather clock standing sentinel in the foyer, it began to chime the hour.

Keeping my head down, I didn't stop until I reached the library.

I closed the door behind me and walked straight back to the chair where I had left my computer.

The room was still in shadows. I picked up the computer and lifted the lid. Opened the Internet tab. But I had no service.

Everything was out. And the battery was in the red zone.

I closed the computer. It had been fully charged before the power outage.

I sat there in the shadows, listening to the orchestra.

It was past time for me to figure out what I was going to do. And now I had even more motivation to do so.

It didn't matter that these things took time. Boucherons landed on their feet. My father's failures were not mine.

I closed my eyes, letting the computer slide to the floor, and tried some of the meditation that was supposed to work wonders.

The rest of the world faded away. It never had worked before. But there was always a first time.

And everything was quiet.

I heard the electricity kick on before I opened my eyes.

Except for the roar of the air conditioning, the house was quiet.

The party that was on the other side of those doors had suddenly gone quiet.

"What the hell?"

I got up and strode to the door. Opened it and stepped into the hallway.

I turned left toward the foyer.

My steps slowed as I reached the grandfather clock.

The silent grandfather clock.

The clock standing sentinel over an empty house.

14

EMMA

I watched James turn and walk past the grandfather clock. Watched him turn right toward the dining room.

I listened to the orchestra playing what was supposed to be happy music.

But there was no happiness inside me. Only devastation.

I turned around and faced the parlor where furniture had been shoved up to the edges of the walls for people to dance. The main ballroom, for reels, was further down, in the next room, but this one was closest to the piano and the little three-man orchestra sitting next to them, so it ended up being a smaller dance floor for waltzes and such.

Ben was walking toward me, making his way around the room.

No. This wasn't right.

I lifted the hem of my skirts, turned, and followed James. I shrugged my arms into the sleeves of his jacket as I walked, enjoying the feeling of it around me. I had his jacket. A tie to him.

I raced past the grandfather clock at what was no doubt a

most unladylike speed and turned right. Then I slowed as I walked down the hallway peeking in each door as I passed, looking for James. I checked the rooms that were lit up for guests first, since it seemed likely that was where he would go.

He wasn't in the men's parlor and he wasn't in the kitchen. So I turned around and retraced my steps. I stopped in front of the library door. It was closed off, signaling to guests not to wander there. Father's desk was there with his important papers, so he understandably didn't want just anyone wandering in. He usually locked the door.

But this was the only place James could have gone.

I slowly turned the doorknob—not locked—and pushed the door open.

If he was in here, he was in darkness. I couldn't see a thing.

I grabbed a lit candle off the nearest sconce and went at it again.

The meager light cast off the shadows as I entered the room.

At first glance, I knew that there was no one there.

Discouraged beyond measure, I dropped into the nearest armchair and set the candle in the little stand next to the chair.

I linked my hands together and rested my chin on them.

He'd said he had to go. Had he literally left the house? I didn't think he meant to actually leave right now. Not this late at night. But maybe he had. The darkness didn't deter men from moving about.

I sighed.

James Boucheron. A mystery man.

I could ask Mother if she knew him, but I really didn't want her attention directed at me right now.

I would ask my brother Martin.

Yes. Feeling encouraged, I straightened up. Martin knew everyone. He would know him or else he would know someone who did.

Someone had to know James or he wouldn't be here to begin with.

Villars had given him clothes to wear, for goodness sakes.

Determined to find my brother, I leaned forward. As I did, my left foot bumped against something.

Thinking a book had fallen off the bookcase, I bent down to pick it up.

Instead, my hands brushed against a thin metal case.

Using both hands, I picked it up. It reminded me a bit of something Sophia and her sisters used all the time.

Whatever it was, they didn't talk about it, but I saw them using it. Anytime I came around, they put it aside, thinking I wouldn't see it, but I had.

This one was different though. It had an image of a half-eaten apple on it. All in a smooth silver.

I opened the case and gasped. It lit up.

Just like the one Sophia owned.

One side lit up and the other side was a bunch of numbers and letters.

I set it so that the side with the numbers was flat in my lap.

Maybe it was something like a piano. Maybe the keys meant something.

I tried tapping some of the letters, but nothing happened.

There was a little row of keys at the top. I tapped one of them and the right side got even brighter.

Intrigued, I pressed another key. Nothing happened. Feeling brave, I tapped the keys randomly like I would play a piano.

At first nothing happened, then the right side of the device changed colors and music began spilling out of it.

I bobbled it, nearly dropping it, but I needed to make it stop.

I didn't know how. I closed it, but that didn't stop it.

It sounded like a group of musicians playing then someone began to sing.

I looked around, panicking.

This was nothing like Sophia's device. I'd never heard any sounds coming from it.

I took it over to the sofa and stuck it between the cushions. There. That helped.

Now I had two people I needed to talk to. Sophia and Martin.

15

JAMES

I stood there, staring at the clock for maybe five minutes. Replaying my encounter with Emma.

So fifteen years ago I had seen a girl playing the piano. I looked to my right. I had, in fact, been standing right about here. I could see the piano from here now. But there was no one sitting there. Neither my father nor Jonathan had seen the girl and I'd only asked them once. I had not wanted them to send me to the psych ward.

I'd tried to let it go, but it had continued to haunt me over the years, mostly in my dreams when I had my guard down.

Now flash forward fifteen years. This had been a more immersive experience. I'd seen the same girl. Only this time she had not been playing the piano. This time she had come alive. We'd talked. And by God, we'd kissed.

I had a good imagination, but that was something even I didn't think my imagination could follow through with. Not in that kind of detail.

Just remembering the feel of Emma's lips on mine had my brain going in the wrong direction. Right now I needed to focus on finding her. And finding out what the hell I had just experienced.

My hands on my hips, I looked at the face of the clock again. Looking for answers. There was a rip between the six and seven. It was barely noticeable, but up close like this, I could see it.

The clock was giving me no answers.

I didn't even know what time it was.

But this seemed like something worthy of waking Jonathan for.

If he was here.

If he was here, he would understand.

I ran a hand through my hair. What made me think he would understand?

I'd just go up. Check on him. Tell him I was worried about him. That was actually true.

And if he just happened to be awake, I'd ask him if he ever thought he heard music.

Satisfied with my plan, I dashed up the stairs and went straight to Jonathan's bedroom.

The door was closed, so I knocked.

I almost thought he wasn't there or he wasn't going to answer.

"Come in."

I blew out a breath of relief and pushed open the door.

The lamp next to his nightstand was on and he was sitting up, wearing his glasses.

"I'm about to go to sleep," I said. "but I wanted to check on you first. See if you needed anything. Since I didn't see Tracie around."

"Come in," he said, motioning to the chair next to his bed. "Have a seat. I was just doing some reading."

Leaving the door open, I went over and sat in the chair he indicated.

Jonathan closed his book and set it aside.

"You look like something might be bothering you."

"Yeah," I said. "I wanted to ask you about something."

Now that I was here, I felt a bit ridiculous. A grown man. Asking about things that didn't exist.

"Anything," Jonathan said. "It gets lonely around here, so I'm glad to have someone to talk to."

"This is an old house," I said. "You must hear some strange noises sometimes."

Jonathan just looked at me.

"What did you hear?" he asked. "I served in Nam, so nothing scares me."

I laughed.

Hell, I thought, I really didn't have anything to lose at this point.

16

EMMA

Although I had planned on talking to Martin first—to find out if he had ever heard of James, I changed my priority. I needed Sophia.

Sophia would know what to do about the box that played music.

Instead of going back through the house, I slipped out through the side door and went right around to the back veranda.

There was a slim possibility that Sophia was here. If she wasn't then it was too late and too dark to go to her house anyway.

I went in through the back door to the kitchen and ran right into Mackenzie. Mackenzie was married to another of my cousins Andrew. The two of them had just recently moved out of here into their own house about a thirty-minute walk from here.

Mackenzie sat with her infant in her arms.

"You brought your baby," I said, a bit surprised.

"I know," she said looking at me sheepishly. "Andrew wanted to talk to someone… I forget his name… who was going to be here and so I came along. We're just going to spend the night."

"It's okay," I said. "I'm actually glad to see you." I gave her a hug, careful not to disturb the sleeping baby.

"How are you?" Mackenzie asked.

"I'm okay," I lied. "Do you know if Sophia is here? I need to ask her about something."

"She's not," Mackenzie said, peaking beneath the blanket at her sleeping baby.

"Oh…" I pressed my hands against the table.

"Something's bothering you," Mackenzie said. "Anything I can do to help?"

I looked at Mackenzie. Sophia's sister.

It suddenly occurred to me that Mackenzie would know how to deal with the device.

"Yes," I said. "I need to show you something."

"Okay. What is it?" Mackenzie asked.

"It's in the library."

"Can you take the baby?" Mackenzie asked.

"Sure." I took the sleeping baby from her arms while she stood up.

"Thank you," she said. "I have trouble standing up with him with this dress and all."

A strange remark. But the Laurent family was rather strange anyway, so I thought nothing of it. I didn't blame them for being strange. Being from New Orleans, they couldn't help it.

Mackenzie and I made our way to the library without incident.

"What's that noise?" Mackenzie asked.

"I didn't know what to do," I said, going to the sofa and pulling out the case.

Mackenzie laid her baby on the sofa and sat down next to him.

"Here," she said, holding out her hands.

She didn't look alarmed at all.

And that troubled me more perhaps more than the device itself.

She opened it and put it on her lap much as I had. She tapped a couple of keys and it went quiet.

I'd been right. She did know how to work it.

"Where did you get this?" she asked, looking up at me.

"I found it. On the floor by that chair." I pointed to the armchair.

She said something noncommittal, then turned her attention back to the device. Tapped some keys, seeming much like I did, but nothing strange happened when she did it.

After a couple of minutes, she closed it and looked at me again.

"Do you know anyone named James Boucheron?" she asked.

17

JAMES

"Do you remember that day fifteen years ago?" I asked.

"Of course," Jonathan said. "You came here for the night with your father."

"Right." He and I had already talked about that. Some of it.

"You asked me about hearing music."

"You remember that?" I sat up straight, something crossed between fear and anticipation washing through me.

"Yes," he said.

"But you said no," I said. "You and Father both said no."

Jonathan nodded.

"But did you?" I asked. "Did you hear it?"

"No," Jonathan said. "I don't hear the music. But I wish I did."

"You know about it," I said softly.

"This house runs deep," Jonathan said. "But I can't see it. Or hear it. I don't carry the blood."

"Then how do you know?" I asked.

"Because everyone else in my family does… or did."

"Everyone?"

"My wife Vaughn, our daughter, Anna. Anna's children. Our son's children." Jonathan removed his glasses and sat back. "The list goes on."

"What are you telling me?"

"Before I tell you," Jonathan said. "Tell me why you're asking."

I had to trust Jonathan. I had to trust someone or else I might go crazy.

"I was downstairs. In the library. I heard music and there was a party. In the house."

I watched Jonathan's expression. Waiting for a reaction of some kind. But he didn't react. He just looked at me and listened.

"You're wondering if I heard anything."

"Did you?"

"Nah," Jonathan shook his head and looked down. "Like I said, I wish I could."

Now that I'd started, I couldn't stop.

"There was a girl. A young lady named Emma."

Jonathan raised an eyebrow.

"You want to see her again."

"Yes," I said before I caught myself. "But… I don't understand. Am I crazy?"

Jonathan steepled his fingers in front of him.

"My wife, Vaughn, was born in the 1700s."

"Wait. What?"

"She was an orphan living with nuns in France. When they decided she was old enough, they sent her to America to be married. She was what they called a casket girl."

"A mail order bride."

"Yes. Except she never made it to her husband."

I swallowed a feeling of dread as Jonathan kept talking.

"Her traveling party was attacked by Indians. She was the only one who survived."

"How?"

"A kind old Indian cast a spell that sent her through time."

I held my breath. Waiting for him to keep going.

"Vaughn became a time traveler."

"Wow," I said. "That's unbelievable." And not a little bit crazy. But at this point, I was in no position to judge or doubt anything.

"But…" Jonathan said. "It didn't stop with her. The spell is passed to everyone who carries her blood in their veins."

"Jonathan," I said. "When Father brought me here…?"

"It was to confirm what he already knew. Your mother was one of my granddaughters."

"I never knew my mother," I said. "Not my real, biological mother."

"I know," Jonathan said.

"You knew this all along?"

"Of course I did."

"But… why didn't you tell me?"

"Ah," Jonathan said, leaning back. "It's not an exact science. There was no guarantee. But when you found your way back here, I was pretty sure it was for a reason."

"What reason?" I asked.

"James," he said. "What are you wearing?"

"I 'um… Villars…" I glanced down at the old-fashioned clothes I was wearing.

Jonathan smiled one of those compassionate smiles. The kind that foretold something painful to come.

"When you heard the music, you were back in time."

I was shaking my head, but I knew he was right.

18

EMMA

Mackenzie was looking at me with an intensity that I found unsettling, to say the least.

"Do you?" she asked. "Do you know him?"

"Maybe," I said, but I was shaking my head. "Why?"

Mackenzie absently adjusted the blanket on her baby, then ran a finger along the edge of the device.

"They've gotten thinner," she said.

"What?"

"Nothing." She squinted and bit her lip. "Emma?"

"What is it?"

"This," she tapped the device. "belongs to a man named James."

"How do you know that?"

"His name is in here."

"Really?" I hadn't seen his name. "Where?"

She opened the device again, but this time it didn't light up.

She groaned. "It just died."

"It died?" I asked, looking warily at the device. "It was alive?"

"No," Mackenzie said, with a small smile. "It lost its energy. It has to be charged."

"Like Sophia's Kindle."

"You know about that?" she asked.

"How could I not?" I asked. "You all are constantly using it."

"That is true," Mackenzie admitted. "Unfortunately… VERY unfortunately. This one can't be fixed."

"Did I break it?" I asked, feeling responsible.

"No." Mackenzie put a hand on my wrist. "I promise. You did not break it."

"Good." I dropped onto the other end of the sofa.

"But," Mackenzie said. "I need you to tell me everything you know about James."

I blushed. I felt the blood as it flooded my cheeks.

"It's okay," Mackenzie smiled. "Whatever it is."

The baby fussed and Mackenzie put a hand on him.

"Villars brought him proper clothes to wear."

"Wait." Mackenzie put up a hand. "Villars brought him clothes?"

"Yes."

She put a hand on the sleeve of my—James's—jacket.

"Would this be one of those items?"

"Yes," I said, unable to keep the little smile from my lips.

"Watch him a minute." Mackenzie stood up, then picked up the candle and, holding it up, looked around the room. She walked around the desk.

"Ah ha," she said, setting the candle down on the desk.

"What is it?" I asked, keeping one hand on the baby to soothe him.

Mackenzie came back around, holding something in her hands.

She sat back on the sofa and held up a pair of denim pants with a leather patch at the waistband. With a quick glance at me, she then held up a gray shirt with a collar and a three-button placket. There was a little pink pony on the left side of the shirt.

Mackenzie closed her eyes and held the shirt to her.

"Mackenzie?" I asked, not sure what was happening.

Her eyes were moist with unshed tears when she opened them.

"I have to tell you something that you won't understand."

"I'm already terribly confused," I said.

"Emma," she said. "James is from the future."

19

JAMES

I stood on the veranda, letting the night air clear my head. I was wearing nothing more than pants and a thin cotton shirt, since I had left my jacket with Emma. That and my jeans and polo shirt.

Since I only had three shirts to my name, I did not find that amusing. Now I had two shirts and this thin white cotton shirt that had to pass as a dress shirt.

The frogs and crickets were setting up quite a racket. Then an owl decided to flutter from limb to limb announcing his presence. The wind rustled the dried leaves, sending them raining from the oak trees. A dog howled in the distance.

So many sounds I didn't hear in the city. Then an old pickup truck with a loud motor passed by on the highway shattering the peacefulness.

The grass still moist from the rain, glistened in the moonlight.

It was somewhere near midnight and the moon was bright overhead.

My thoughts were so tangled I could barely make sense of them.

But no matter which direction they went, they kept ending up back at Emma. The way she smelled, like magnolias and daffodils. The way she fit perfectly in my arms. Her skin so soft. Her lips even softer. And the way she had responded to my kiss.

I think she may never have been kissed before.

But she wasn't real. She was someone in the past.

I absently stuck my hands in my pockets, only to find Emma's silk glove that I had stashed in there.

Pulling it out, I ran it through my hands, remembering everything all over again.

I had her glove and she had my jacket.

Jonathan hadn't said it, but I'd gotten the impression that me going back in the past didn't just happen at random. He seemed to think that it happened for a reason.

That soul mates could connect through time. Vaughn apparently was the exception, since she never stayed more than a few years with Jonathan in this time.

It was *those of her blood* that traveled through time.

The fact that I was related to Jonathan was just another piece of information that I had to absorb.

But right now… right now I needed a drink.

I'd promised myself that I would not drink any kind of alcohol until I had my feet back under me. The stigma of a homeless drunk was too much.

But I was here at the Becquerel Estate. I was in a safe place. Not on the streets.

I went back inside, passed by the silent grandfather clock, the silent piano, and went into the library.

Going straight to the liquor cabinet, I poured myself a whiskey, then went in search of my computer.

Now, damn it, instead of looking for ways to get back on my feet, I was going to be researching the history of this house.

And seeing what I could find about time travel in general.

The computer wasn't on the desk and it wasn't on the chair.

I looked everywhere for it. Since it was technically Jonathan's computer, I was getting a little bit worried. Maybe he had come downstairs for it.

But I stood there shaking my head. When I'd left him, he was falling asleep. He wasn't the kind of man to get up the middle of the night and go in search of his computer.

Okay. I sat down in the armchair. Where had I last seen it?

I had been sitting right here…

Good God.

I had left the computer in the past. Along with my jeans and my favorite polo shirt.

And quite possibly my heart.

20

EMMA

The next morning I woke to the normal sounds of chickens and dogs barking.

The scent of coffee, bacon, and biscuits drifting from the kitchen outside.

I stretched beneath the sheets. It was a normal day…

Except that it wasn't.

James.

My whole world had turned upside down last night.

First James. A man I had never met before had turned me inside out. A stranger in the night who'd stolen a kiss. Not just a kiss, but my first kiss.

I pressed my fingertips to my lips, remembering the feel of lips his against mine.

Pulling my thoughts away from there for a moment, I replayed my conversation with Mackenzie. She had known that James was from the future.

And before Andrew had come looking for her, I'd learned that Mackenzie, too, was from the future, too.

When I thought about it, really thought about it, it all made perfect sense.

The pieces slid together like a puzzle.

And not only was Mackenzie from the future, so was Sophia, and their brother Cameron, and their other sister Victoria.

Four siblings, all from the future, had married my four cousins.

I sat up and put my feet on the cool floor.

Laurents, all of them, and the Laurents from New Orleans had always been a little bit strange.

Everyone excused them, though, because they were from New Orleans. But now to learn that they were all from the future put a whole new spin on things.

Mackenzie had called the device I'd found a computer. She said it was like the Kindle, only it could do more things. But she had no way to make it run again. Essentially, it was worthless in this time period.

I slid my feet into a pair of slippers and padded over to the water pitcher. I poured water into the basin and splashed cool water on my face.

Wiping my face with a towel, I walked over to the window and looked down across the lawn toward the road canopied by oaks. If I pressed my cheek to the glass, I could just see the gazebo off to my left.

Some of the guests would have stayed overnight. Most of them actually.

I still didn't know if James had stayed overnight or if he had left.

Mackenzie had suggested that James had done neither. She believed that he had traveled through time. Back to his own time.

If he had, would he come back?

Would he come back here, to me? He'd said he had some things to take care of first.

I have some things I have to figure out before I can be here. I have to go.

But he didn't know if he would be back or not.

But he'd kissed me and held me close like he never wanted to leave.

There was one thing and only one thing I was sure of.

If he had gone to the future, he had taken my heart with him.

21

JAMES

Without a computer, I had gone to the books. Jonathan had an extensive library.

I found two books about time travel, with highlighted and earmarked pages. I wasn't the only person to have gone searching for answers in here.

None of what I read helped me, though.

I'm not even sure what I was looking for.

There were a lot of theories about whether or not it was possible.

"You hungry?" Jonathan asked, coming to the door. "It's lunch time."

"Sure." I followed him to the kitchen and we had grilled cheese sandwiches that Tracie made.

Tracie wasn't looking at me suspiciously anymore. She seemed to have accepted that I was going to be here for awhile.

"Have you found anything yet?" Jonathan asked.

"No," I said, with a glance at Tracie. "I seem to have... misplaced your computer."

"Oh," he said. "Well that's been known to happen on occasion."

Tracie was filling the dishwasher and didn't appear to be paying any mind to our conversation.

"I'll order another one."

He pulled his cell phone out of his pocket. Tapped a couple of keys.

Then made a face and slid the phone over to me.

"You order it," he said, pulling out his wallet and handing me a credit card.

Tracie noticed us now and watched me with raised eyebrows.

"Sure," I said. "Same kind?"

"Whatever you think," he said. "I don't keep up with all that. Victoria ordered the last one."

"Your granddaughter?" I asked.

"Yes. The last one who went… out of the country."

That was about as good a metaphor as any, I guess. I wondered just how much Tracie really knew. It was hard to live in the house with someone and not know something about what was going on in their lives, especially when people kept disappearing.

Fifteen minutes later, I had a new computer on the way and slid Jonathan's credit card back to him.

What Tracie didn't know was that there was no way I would ever steal anything from Jonathan. It was hard enough for me to accept room and board. And I could only do that because I knew I was helping him out.

"Anything in particular you would like for me to work on today?" I asked.

"Nah," he said. "Just keep doing that research you're doing." He sat back. "Actually, after we finish eating, I'd like to show you something."

After lunch I followed Jonathan back to the library. He shifted some books around, then pulled out a large Bible. The family Bible.

He handed it to me.

"You might find what you're looking for in here." Then he turned around and headed for the door. "I'm going to take a nap," he said over his shoulder.

With a little laugh, I sat down at the desk and opened the Bible—to the middle section to the handwritten pages.

The one thing I noticed was that there were a lot of names written off to the sides, in the margins, as though they had been afterthoughts.

I saw Vaughn's name in there twice. One with Jonathan, as expected, and again with a man named Nathaniel Becquerel.

Vaughn had been married to two men?

Then I found Emma Becquerel's name.

There was a name out beside it.

I pulled the page closer. No.

James Boucheron.

I sat back in the chair. I did not have a common name. And there were no other Boucherons in the list. Did this mean I had married Emma? In the past. Or was my name there for another reason?

It was then that I realized what I was looking for.

I was looking for a way to get back.

I didn't want to make a new start here. In the modern world.

I wanted to make a new start in the past. With Emma.

Surely that was possible. Others had done it.

Besides, the proof was right here in front of me.

I didn't know how much I believed in fate. I'd never given it much thought.

But I did know that I had been haunted by the girl who could be none other than Emma Becquerel since I was fifteen years old.

22

EMMA

One week later

I sat at the piano, pecking at the keys, not even bothering to play a tune. My heart wasn't in it and hadn't been in it. Not all week.

I spent my time watching for James. Hoping he would come back.

I'd talked some more to Mackenzie before she and Andrew had gone home. But I hadn't learned anything that had been helpful.

She'd just confirmed what I already knew. She and her siblings were from the future.

They had been drawn to the past to be with their soul mates.

She hadn't told me much more. I don't know if she didn't know much more or if she didn't want to tell me much more. Either way, I was still confused about… well… everything.

If there was so much time travel going on, why hadn't someone told me about it?

I was actually a little miffed that I'd been left out of the loop.

If I found out my brother knew about it, I was going to be even more upset.

Martin, as my brother, was obligated to tell me things like this. Especially now that I was part of it.

Mother swept into the parlor, wearing her favorite green day dress, and sat down in her chair in front of the fireplace.

After a moment, she looked over at me.

"Come sit by me," she said.

This was different. No complaints about me not practicing and an invitation to sit next to her before my hour of practice time was up.

I went over and sat in the chair next to hers. She raised a brow when she saw that I wearing one of my favorite dress—a silver gown with a hoop skirt that was little too wide for every day. I'd been wearing my favorite dresses all week. Just in case.

"I haven't had a chance to really talk to you since the ball," she said.

"I know," I said. I'd been rather avoiding her for one thing and for another, she'd been busy with other guests who had stayed more than just one night.

"Did you get a chance to meet the young Dr. White?" She asked the question almost as though we were picking up the last conversation we'd had at the ball.

"No," I shook my head.

"Hmm." Mother concentrated on her needlepoint. Digging in the basket of yarn and thread between us, I picked up an embroidery loop someone had left unfinished and distracted myself by looking for the pattern they were going for.

"I didn't see you on the dance floor," Mother said.

"No ma'am."

"Where were you?"

I let the embroidery loop fall into my lap. So much for concentration.

This was the question I had been expecting, but oddly enough I didn't hear judgement in her tone. I thought I actually detected concern.

"I wasn't feeling well," I said, "so I went up to bed." That wasn't a lie. After my time with James and my conversation with Mackenzie, that was exactly what I had done.

"Someone saw you sitting on the swing with a young man." Mother didn't even bat an eye when she said this.

I kept my gaze down. Picked up the loop and ran the thread that was already there through the canvas. If it was wrong, too bad. They shouldn't have left unfinished work lying around.

"For a moment," I said.

"Who was he?"

"James." I couldn't lie to my mother. I didn't have it in me. Besides, I didn't want to. I didn't want to lie about him. I wanted to tell everyone about him. Yet at the same time, there was no way they could understand. What I felt for James was so strong… so real… that it affected me all the way through.

Everything I thought about involved James in some way. Not just questions about whether or not he would come back, but I thought about what a future with him might look like. We could have babies like Mackenzie and Sophia had with their husbands.

"Emma?" Mother said, getting my attention.

"Yes?" I looked up at her.

"I know you're not a child anymore. I know you're an adult and that you'll be getting married soon and moving away."

"Mother—"

"It's okay," she continued. "It's the way it's supposed to be. A woman goes away with her man. Just as I came here with your father. You have to make your own way in life."

I already knew what she was telling me. I'd watched my cousins and the women they had married.

But what Mother didn't know was that the man I loved wasn't from this time. I couldn't go away with him because I couldn't get to him.

"Mother," I said. "How much do you know about the time travel?"

"The time—"

"The Becquerels," I said. "and the time travel."

"Well," she said, looking at me sideways, her fingers lying still in her lap. "I know quite a bit, actually."

I gaped at my mother.

"Why didn't you tell me?" I asked.

"You didn't ask," Mother said with a little smile.

23

JAMES

After roaming the house aimlessly for the rest of the day, I'd approached Jonathan with the idea of doing some painting. Just one of the many projects I had in mind to do around here.

We worked it out and I took his truck into town to pick up some paint. In spite of Tracie's unstated misgivings, I took Jonathan's credit card. It was rather sweet, really, how she watched out for him.

I was glad he had her.

I went straight to the hardware store and ordered the paint. Then I had some time to kill before it would be ready.

I entertained myself by roaming the store looking at all the gadgets. There weren't many people in the store, so I basically had it to myself.

There was a new electronic laser level that recorded measurements. I played with that for a while and if I'd had any money to my name, I would have bought one for myself. Not that I was planning on building anything, but it was cool nonetheless.

When it was time, I went back to the paint counter.

A silver-haired older woman approached me.

"Excuse me," she said. "I don't mean to be intrusive, but that looks like Jonathan Becquerel's truck."

Spending most of my life in the city, my first instinct was to protect Jonathan and not tell her anything. But I reminded myself that this was a small southern town and everyone knew everyone.

"It is," I said. "I'm just doing some errands for him."

"Is he alright?" she asked. "I haven't seen him in such a long time. Neigh onto two years, if I remember correctly."

"That's a long time," I said, watching as the clerk put my paint in a cart for me to take outside to the truck. "But he's doing okay."

"Good," she said.

"You know him well?" I asked.

"Oh yes." She leaned forward and lowered her voice. "We were high school sweethearts."

"You don't say." I looked at her in a different light. She looked about Jonathan's age and she'd done a nice job of keeping herself looking nice.

"You should come out and visit him," I said.

"Really? Maybe I will."

"I'll tell him I saw you, Mrs…"

"Oh," she said. "I'm Miss Ophelia Burton. I never married."

"I'll tell him we talked, Miss Burton," I said. "It was a pleasure meeting you."

As I loaded the paint in the back of the truck, I rolled my eyes at myself. Had I really just invited a stranger to come see Jonathan?

The small town culture was rubbing off on me and I'd barely been here any time at all.

Still, it was sweet to think that Jonathan had a high school sweetheart who had never married. I climbed into the cab and started the motor.

Maybe she hadn't married because she'd never gotten over him.

It was possible.

And now I'd met Emma, I actually understood how that could happen.

When the heart made its choice, the heart never forgot.

24

EMMA

Mother and I walked outside among the flowers. Roses. Magnolias. The daffodils were my favorite. Not because they were yellow, but because they smelled so good.

If I had my way, we'd have them all over the house, but Mother rarely let anyone cut them. She claimed they lasted so much longer outside and if we wanted to smell them, we could walk in the garden.

"Tell me what you know, Mother." I could barely wait any longer for her to get around to telling me what she knew.

"I guess I'll just cut to the chase," she said. "Your father is from the future."

I stopped and gaped at her.

Surely I had not heard her correctly.

"Wait a minute. Father is from the future? Father time traveled to be here? Then that means…"

I couldn't say the words. But I couldn't not say them.

"That means I can time travel."

"Maybe," Mother said without a hitch.

"Oh my God." I could barely catch my breath.

"Language," Mother said, but without her usual sternness.

"Mother." I was practically dancing a circle around her.

"Not necessarily," she said. "Your Aunt Margaret was a Becquerel and she didn't time travel. Nor did any of her children."

"But they married people who did."

"Yes."

I stood still and put a hand on my forehead.

"This is too complicated," I said. "it makes my head hurt."

"Don't let it," Mother said. "You're thinking about it too much."

"Mackenzie thinks that James is from the future," I blurted.

"James is your beau?"

"I don't know if he's my beau," I said, walking slowly now. "I don't know if I'll ever even see him again."

"Can I make a suggestion?"

"Of course."

"If you don't believe it, it won't happen."

I stopped. Bent over to breathe in the scent of a daffodil.

"Do you believe that?" I asked.

"Yes."

I looked at my mother. She was suddenly someone I didn't know. The cross, stern woman had morphed into someone kind and understanding.

"So it's that simple?"

Mother slipped a pair of scissors out of her pocket, cut off a daffodil at the stem, and handed it to me.

"It's that simple," she said. "And that hard."

I held the flower in my hand.

I literally felt like my world had turned upside down.

My mother had cut one of her flowers and handed it to me.

And she was telling me that in order to see James again, I just had to believe.

25

JAMES

I spent the next six days painting. Painting the tall white columns required climbing up on a ladder, but I did it. Then I painted the rest from the second-floor balcony. Anything higher than that would have to wait.

I painted the railings. Tedious, exhausting work.

But it kept my mind off of things. Emma mostly.

Jonathan seemed to think that there was a key to the clock that could be used to travel through time, but he didn't have it. Didn't know where it was.

Other than that, he insisted that storms had something to do with the time travel. And I remembered that it had been raining that night I'd met Emma. The night of the ball.

If the time travel was supposed to bring soul mates together, then why had it introduced me to Emma only to pull me back here?

I sat back on my heels and looked toward the river.

There was a car coming down the oak canopied lane. A white SUV actually. I watched as it slowly made its way down the lane and parked next to the house in the circle drive.

Jonathan didn't get a lot of visitors. Tracie was really the only one who came and went.

The mailman drove up here once a day and one of the delivery services had dropped off the new computer this morning. I knew how I'd be spending my evening. Setting up Jonathan's computer.

It was the least I could do considering that I had left his other one somewhere in the past.

The driver's door opened and an older woman stepped out.

Wow. It was Miss Ophelia Burton. Jonathan's high school sweetheart that I'd met at the hardware store.

She was rather stunning for a woman in her seventies. She didn't look a day over forty-five to me.

Standing up, I wiped my hands on a towel and went to meet her at the top of the stairs.

"Hi," I said with a smile.

"Hi."

"Come on up here." I motioned with my hands. "I'll let Jonathan know you're here."

"You know," she said. "I was shy in high school. Jonathan and I dated some, but I never let him know how I really felt. So I thought I'd let him know this time around."

"Good for you," I said, leading her inside.

"We're not getting any younger."

When she wiped her hands on her skirt, I could see that they were trembling. She was nervous as a schoolgirl.

I wiped a grin from my face.

"You can wait here," I said. "or in the parlor."

"I'll just wait here," she said.

"Don't go anywhere," I said, then turned and sprinted up the stairs.

"Jonathan," I called. But he wasn't here. Wasn't in his room.

I went back downstairs.

"Did I come at a bad time?" Ophelia asked.

"No. No. I'll find him."

I went around to the study and found him there, stretched out on the sofa, reading a book.

The man definitely needed something else to do.

"There's someone here to see you," I said.

Jonathan sat up, pulling his glasses off, and setting the book aside.

"Who is it?"

"I don't know her," I said. I didn't want to take away the surprise aspect of Ophelia being here.

"Okay," he said and together we walked down the hallway toward the foyer.

At first I thought she'd left, but then I saw her standing next to the grandfather clock.

Jonathan froze and just looked at her.

She smiled.

"Ophelia?" Jonathan said.

"Hello Jonathan," she said, taking a step toward him.

He held out his arms and she walked into them.

I felt like I'd just witnessed a miracle.

Two people who hadn't seen each other in probably fifty years. They recognized each other immediately and apparently that bond was still there.

Jonathan had been married for years and years. He had children and grandchildren with Vaughn, yet he never forgot his high school sweetheart.

It was not only heartwarming, but it also gave me hope. Hope that even if years passed, Emma and I could be reunited.

26

EMMA

Two days later I stood in front of the grandfather clock, staring at its face as it steadily ticked away the minutes.

There was a key in the lock behind the glass door. I think maybe Mackenzie and her sisters knew what purpose it held. That it was somehow one of the secrets to the time travel, but they weren't telling.

Maybe they didn't believe it or maybe they just didn't trust me to know what to do with the information.

"Are you ready to go?" Mother asked, coming down the stairs, in one of her flowing ball gowns, already wearing her long, hooded cloak over it.

Technically I was ready. I was dressed in one of my finer ball gowns, this one a new crimson silk dress. It was probably the most beautiful dress I'd ever owned.

I pulled on my wool cloak and fastened it at the neck.

"Yes," I said. But I did not want to go. Tonight's ball was being held at Doc White's house. A holiday ball. Hopefully the last of the season, though that could change at a moment's notice.

It was, however, the first ball the Whites had ever held, at least to my knowledge. And even though I had used the younger Doc White's name as a place holder on my dance card at my own family's ball, I had never met him. I didn't even know if he ever showed up that night or not. Didn't care.

All I wanted to do was to curl up with a good book in front of the fireplace and daydream about James.

But, of course, that would be ridiculous.

A girl could not live off memories alone, especially not with a mother like mine.

She told me to believe in James, but at the same time, she told me to live my life.

I had a bit of trouble with the inconsistencies of thought.

At any rate, I would go to tonight's ball.

Knowing that I had to endure the evening, I went outside onto the veranda with Mother.

Wolves or maybe dogs were howling in the distance, their lonely wails lingering on the cold early evening air.

The clouds were banked and even though I didn't have a lot of experience with snow, I thought they looked a lot like snow clouds. And it was certainly cold enough. But since no one else seemed to be concerned, I didn't say anything.

"Where's Father?" I asked. Father was supposed to be here with the carriage to pick us up. Maybe he was trying to find a driver.

"I don't know," Mother said, pulling her warm cloak more tightly around her.

Travel in the winter was not something I wanted to do and I had trouble seeing the point really. But the worst of winter would be setting in after the holidays and people wanted to gather.

A gust of wind blew at my hair. I would have done just as well to have saved the hour it took to get my hair just right.

Maybe Father had changed his mind. Maybe we weren't going after all.

"There he is," Mother said with relief.

As we climbed inside the carriage, I wondered if Mother went through life worried that Father would suddenly vanish into another time.

He was a Becquerel so it did seem to be possible.

Anything was possible.

27

JAMES

Ophelia stayed for dinner. I'd already planned on making salad and baked potatoes, so I just added another potato to the oven and another bowl of salad.

Jonathan and Ophelia sat in the parlor, catching up over a glass of wine.

I wondered just how long it had been since this old house had heard so much laughter.

I poured myself a glass of wine and went back into the library. My new favorite room. I spent some time setting up the new computer. It had gotten surprisingly easy since the last time I set up another new computer.

Then I searched around on the Internet a bit, but I wasn't feeling any interest in it, so I shut it down and plucked a book off the shelf.

Settling on the sofa with my glass of wine and my book, I found my thoughts wandering away from the pages of the book to Emma.

Was she here in this very house at this very moment? But in a different timeline?

Despite the relaxing effects of the wine, I felt edgy. Like I needed to be doing something, but I didn't know what that something was.

Grabbing the computer, I typed in today's date. But changed the year to 1858.

It took some searching, but I found an obscure article, a journal actually, that listed the dates and some corresponding noticeable events.

December 8, 1858. Nothing.

But on December 9, I found a newspaper entry someone had posted.

A rare snow storm severely injures Becquerel family of three and their driver. Fate unknown.

"That's it?" I asked out loud. I looked for something else, but found no follow up.

I set the computer back on the coffee table.

This was not helping matters.

There was no way for me to control what happened in the past.

There was no way to control the time travel. Not unless I was able to somehow manipulate the weather.

I leaned my head back against the sofa and closed my eyes, keeping my breathing slow and steady.

The night wind howled around the house and a limb slammed against the window.

But still I managed to keep my thoughts calm.

The steady ticking of the grandfather clock lulled me into a doze. Then the clock began to chime the hour.

I almost forgot to breath.

The grandfather clock.

Had Ophelia known how to fix it? I'd specifically asked Jonathan about it. He said it had been broken for years. They quit making parts for it and there were none to be had.

I opened my eyes and slowly stood up. The room was in darkness.

I instinctively put a hand on the coffee table for my computer. It wasn't there.

With no other light source, I got up and carefully made my way toward the door.

Slowly pushing the door open, I listened for Jonathan and Ophelia. But I couldn't hear them.

That could mean so many things. Including her expressing her feelings for him.

There were a couple of candles scattered along the walls, casting a soft glow along the hallway.

I continued toward the foyer. Drawn by the clock.

By the time I reached the clock, the chiming had stopped, its echo hanging in the air. It was just ticking.

And I knew.

I was no longer in my time.

28

EMMA

We had no more arrived at the White's house, than the ball was cancelled.

One the White's staff approached the driver as soon as we arrived. We could hear them talking, but their words were muffled.

The staff member walked off and we waited while our driver, Virgil, climbed down and opened the door. He was bundled in his wool coat, but his nose was red from the cold.

"What is it Virgil?" Father asked, "what's going on?"

"Dr. White said everybody who lives nearby should go on back home," he said.

"What's happened?" Father asked.

"The weather," he said. "Dr. White doesn't want you all to get stuck here with the storm coming in."

"Can we make it back?" Mother asked Father. "It's already dark."

I looked outside. I'd been right. Big fluffy snowflakes were falling like raindrops outside the carriage. So they had been snow clouds. I should have said something.

"We can't stay here?" I asked, feeling trepidation about traveling in this cold weather.

"It's only an hour," Father said. "Dr. White is probably right. Once the roads freeze over, it could be days before we can get home again."

I nodded. The thought of having to stay here for days with a bunch of strangers who couldn't travel was far more unsettling than just going home. At home, we had plenty of firewood to keep us warm through the storm. I'd much rather be snowed in at home than here.

Father apparently agreed.

"Take us home, Virgil," he said.

"Yes, Sir." Virgil said, closed the door, and climbed back up on his seat.

"We should have known," Mother said, looking at Father. "Do you think they'll ever get to the point where they can predict the weather?"

"Maybe." Father just shrugged and turned to gaze out the window.

If he was from the future, as Mother said, then he was really good at hiding it.

I wanted to ask him about it, but Mother shook her head just enough to warn me against it. I didn't understand this and probably never would.

Maybe they had agreed not to talk about it.

I settled back in my seat and snuggled into my cloak. At least I'd gotten what I wanted. Sort of. I was getting to go home.

We'd been riding for about fifteen minutes when we came to a bridge over a little tributary that ran into the Mississippi River. It was barely a waterway at all, dried up half the time.

The carriage stopped.

Father waited a minute, then stuck his head out the window.

"What's wrong, Virgil?"

"Looks awfully slick, Sir," Virgil said.

"It'll be alright," Father said. "The temperature isn't cold enough for it to freeze."

"You want me to cross it?" Virgil asked.

"It's the only way to get home," Father said, then pulled his head back inside and closed the little window.

"How do you know, Father?" I asked.

He turned and looked at me and for a moment I thought he was actually going to answer. That he was going to tell me something useful. Something maybe about him being from the future.

But as the front carriage wheels hit the bridge, I grabbed hold of the seat.

Something seems wrong.

Then the back wheels hit the bridge and I knew something wasn't wrong. Everything was.

The carriage was sliding.

Mother gasped and grabbed hold of Father. Father was gripping a handle on the side of the carriage.

It all happened so fast, I didn't really have time to process what was happening.

All I knew was that I was being thrown from my seat and the whole carriage was turning on its side.

29

JAMES

The big old house was quiet. Nothing but the steady ticking of the grandfather clock to keep the shadows from the candle light company.

It was such a marked difference from the night I was here during the party.

I walked into the parlor and stopped in front of the piano. I smiled at the memory of Emma—I was certain it was her—playing and playing badly.

"Can I help you, Sir?" I turned at the sound of Villars' voice.

The man stood behind me.

"Villars," I said. "Do you know where Emma is?"

"Emma isn't here." Villars was looking at me sideways. "Are you supposed to be here?"

"I don't know." I stuck my hands in my pockets.

"Do you know when she'll be back?"

"No, Sir," Villars said, with a glance toward the window. "What with the weather and all."

"The weather?" I went to the window and, shoving the velvet drapes aside, looked outside.

Snow was coming down like confetti.

It was beautiful.

But snow in Natchez?

If she was out in this…

I turned and pinned Villars with my gaze.

"Is she out in this weather?"

"They went to the White's ball. Dr. White."

The Whites. Why was that name familiar?

"It's only about an hour from here," he added. "They'll be home tonight."

"They?" I needed to sit down.

Part of my brain was trying to tell me something and the other part was trying not to listen.

"Mr. and Mrs. Becquerel. And Emma."

A party of three.

"Did they have a driver?" I asked.

"Excuse me. A driver?

"Yes," I said, impatient now. "A driver. Did they have a driver?"

"Of course."

I dropped into the closet armchair.

"Villars," I said. "I need to ask you something that is very important."

"Yes Sir. I understand, Sir."

"What is today's date?"

"December 8."

I made a motion for him to continue. "The year. What's the year?"

"1858."

A rare snow storm severely injures Becquerel family of three and their driver. Fate unknown.

"Villars," I said. "I need your help."

30

EMMA

My head was pressed against the ceiling and my feet were in a puddle of water. Ice cold water.

I didn't know if I had passed out or not. I don't think I did, but all I could remember was the rolling of the carriage. It seemed to roll in slow motion.

"Mother? Father?"

No one answered and it was dark. I tried to move, but my foot was caught.

I reached out, trying to find Mother or Father. But there was nothing but empty space.

I lay very still for a moment, forcing myself to think. To remember.

We had been traveling in the snow storm. When we had gotten to the bridge, we had started sliding.

The bridge must have been iced over. And Virgil would not have known to watch for ice. It was so rarely really cold here that how could he possibly know?

Like us, he was accustomed to hot weather. He'd probably never even driven a carriage in the snow and ice before.

I called out to my parents again and tried to pull my foot free.

The skirt of my new crimson colored dress was soaked. Ruined.

It didn't matter.

It mattered that I couldn't find my parents.

I called out to Virgil.

Silence.

My breath hitched.

Oh God. What if they had all been killed?

They had been killed and I was left to freeze to death at the bottom of this river.

No. No. That couldn't be.

The carriage shifted and slid a few feet.

Then I heard someone calling my name.

"I'm here!" I said. "Down here."

My eyes suddenly filled with tears. Someone was going to get me out of here.

I wasn't going to die down here in the dark riverbed with my foot locked beneath wheel.

"Emma!"

But he was walking past me.

He couldn't hear me. I was trapped down here at the edge of the river in the water and no one could find me.

I had to get out of here. I bent over and began tugging at whatever was holding my foot trapped.

It was too much. I twisted my foot to no avail. And the water was getting deeper.

What had happened to everyone?

Where had they gone?

I called out again.

But the only answer I got was the sound of the river rushing past the carriage wheel.

There had to be a way out of here. I just needed to think.
But I was so very cold. So cold I couldn't think.
Maybe I would just rest a few minutes.

31

JAMES

I was not the most practiced horse rider, but this horse—the stable boy said his name was Skye Traveler—could take care of both of us.

Villars had given me directions to the White's home. I don't know how he knew. Even though he never seems to leave the house, Villars seemed to know just about everything.

The road was illuminated by the glow of the moon through the falling snow.

Besides that, it was dark. Dark and cold. Unseasonably cold.

The falling snow in the trees was beautiful. Beautiful but deadly.

Even though the snow was barely more than a dusty layer on the ground, the puddles on the road were starting to freeze. I worried about Skye Traveler sliding on the new ice, but he seemed adept at walking around them.

The moon reflected off the Mississippi River, so wide it looked like an ocean from here.

Following the directions, I turned right after a mile and the road narrowed even more.

The only sounds were the horse's hooves steadily thumping

on the ground and the squeaking of the leather saddle beneath me.

For the first time since I'd left the Becquerel Estate, it occurred to me that I didn't have a gun. I was out here all alone and had no protection.

I focused on my task. Get to the White's house, find Emma and her parents. Make sure they were safe.

Prevent them from being victims of the storm.

I'd come back now for a reason. I could think of no better reason than protecting Emma.

I came to a bridge and stopped.

I'd been around enough to recognize the sheen of ice on an overpass.

This could most definitely be a problem. One I hadn't considered. I couldn't put myself and Skye Traveler at risk.

I slid off the horse's back and held his reins loosely in my hands as I walked up to the bridge and looked around.

That's when I heard voices.

Following the voices, I walked left following the riverbank.

Up ahead, there was a woman huddled over a man, both on the ground.

The woman looked over her shoulder and I saw a tinge of relief beneath the fear on her face.

"Mrs. Becquerel?" I asked, walking cautiously toward them. "I'm James. I'm here to help."

As I came closer, I saw tears running down her cheeks.

"My husband's leg is broken," she said. "And our daughter is still down there."

"Emma," I breathed. "Where is she?"

"I don't know. Our carriage went off the bridge. Virgil got Samuel up here, but…" She turned back to her husband. "I can't leave him."

"I will find her," I said, tying the horse's reins around a low tree limb.

"Virgil is looking for her," she said, but I was already headed back toward the bridge, walking through the snow.

The beautiful, deadly snow that dusted everything.

If the carriage had gone off the bridge, I needed to start there.

I would find Emma.

I would find her if it was the last thing I did.

32

EMMA

"Emma. Emma. Wake up."

"No," I murmured. "I don't want to."

I just wanted to go back to sleep. I was warm here under my wool cloak.

Somewhere in the back of my mind, I recognized that my foot was loose, but I didn't care.

I drifted off again.

Then a man's arms were around me, lifting me up.

I put my arm around his neck and rested my cheek against his chest.

He smelled good. Familiar. A deep woodsy scent with undertones of lavender.

Safe. I was safe.

Safe enough that I could go back to sleep.

As the man carried me up the ravine, out of the water, to the safety of the riverbank, I imagined that my savior was James.

"Not possible," I murmured to myself.

The man kissed me on the top of my head.

"Anything is possible if you just believe it, my love," he said.

James.

He sounded like James. That voice. Deep and soothing.

I smiled against his chest.

"You're safe now," he said. "Don't worry."

I closed my eyes and fell asleep in his arms.

When I woke the next time, I was on a cot in front of a fireplace.

I didn't recognize the place. It smelled odd. Like food cooking. It smelled like a kitchen.

I opened my eyes just enough to see the flames in the fireplace. I was still cold, but the blankets were dry and warm.

I caught sight of my beautiful crimson dress lying on the back of a chair next to the fireplace. Ruined. It was ruined now.

There were so many things I needed to think about. To sort out. But I didn't have the energy.

I'd been in an accident.

Trapped. But someone had gotten me out.

I imagined it was James, but, of course, that was only my imagination.

I had to move on. Tuck James among the memories in the back of my mind. Mother insisted that I allow other men to court me now.

Too old. She said I was getting too old to wait much longer.

I needed to have babies. And only a young woman could have babies.

Men would only marry young ladies.

I knew I was getting older. I felt older. Especially today.

I just needed to go back to sleep.

To take a nap.

Then I could think about everything. Sort it all out.

Figure out how I was going to live the rest of my life without James in it.

James. My eyes teared up.

He was the man I loved.

The only man I would ever love.

It didn't matter if I had to marry another. James was the one who had my heart.

Even if I never saw him again.

33

JAMES

I was incredibly busy the rest of the night.

It wasn't until the dawn broke over the horizon that I took a minute to sit and rest.

I used all my skills as a CEO to orchestrate taking care of three people who had been in a horrible accident. And I did it with very few resources.

This was 1858. There were no emergency responders to call. I had to do it all myself.

It just validated that my family's company had not fallen due to anything I had done. It had fallen because of a series of bad decisions and just plain bad luck.

I was more confident now than I had been in some time that I could get myself back on track to being successful again.

But the important thing was that I had found Emma in time to pull her out of the river.

I'd gotten her parents on the back of a wagon and sent them back to Dr. White's home. He seemed best qualified to treat her father's broken leg and Eloise wasn't leaving his side.

I still didn't know where the driver, Virgil, was, but I hadn't given up on finding him. He'd been there to pull

Samuel and Eloise out of the river, so I had faith that he would show up.

But I was the one who had dislodged Emma's foot and pulled her from the river. She'd been on her way to hypothermia and I wasn't sure she was out of the woods yet.

So I stayed by her side. With the help of Eloise, I'd found a little unoccupied cabin and started a fire. All those years being a boy scout weren't wasted after all.

My father had always said that a man could never know too much. You would never know when you might need to know something. More truer words had ever been spoken.

As I sat beside Emma, watching her breathe, I realized that part of what had been holding me back was thinking I had to do something that would please my father.

But I did not. My father was longer here. I was the one I had to please. My success depended on me and no one else.

And right now I needed to figure how to adapt to living and working in the nineteenth century.

I was not a historian, but I did know that all hell was about to break loose in the country. Surely there was something I could do now that would be useful during the conflict to come.

It was something I would have to explore, because if I had anything to do with it, there was no way I was going to leave Emma again.

I hadn't done anything to get myself back here—to travel through time. Maybe I was here simply because she needed me.

I could think of no better reason, really.

Saving a damsel in distress had always been one of my fantasies. And Emma was more than just a damsel in distress. She was the one I wanted to spend the rest of my life with.

All I had to do now was to convince her to agree to that.

Her and her parents.

So I was back to needing prospects for a future in the 1800s. Her parents would want a man with prospects for their daughter. Not just someone who seemed to be no more than a drifter.

Emma stirred and opened her eyes.

I knelt next to her and put a hand on her forehead. Her skin was warm, but not hot.

"James?" she whispered.

"Yes, my love." Holding up her head, I brought a glass of water to her lips and waited while she drank.

"Just go back to sleep," I said. "Get some rest."

She closed her eyes and soon she was breathing steadily again.

34

EMMA

I dreamed about James. I dreamed he was here with me. Taking care of me.

My dreams had been vivid. His startling blue eyes watching me. His hand sweeping lightly across my forehead.

And his soothing voice comforting me.

I'd gone back to sleep, only to dream of him. Dreaming of sitting on the porch swing with him. Kissing him.

When I woke this time, I was more alert. Alive again.

"Good morning, beautiful," James said.

James?

Surely I was dreaming again.

I turned my head, looking over my shoulder.

Oh my. It really was James. He was here. I hadn't imagined it after all.

"How are you here?" I asked.

He shrugged. "I don't know. The fates of time brought me back to you and, it seemed, just in the nick of time."

"The fates of time?" I asked, with a little smile.

"It's good to have you back among the living." He slid from the chair to kneel in front of me.

I nodded. "What happened?"

"What do you remember?"

I pressed a hand against my forehead. My wrist was sore. In fact, I might just be sore all over.

"The carriage," I said. "We slid off the bridge."

I put a hand on his shoulder. "My parents?" A feeling of dread spilled over me.

"They're okay. I put them on a wagon back to Dr. White's house." I took her hand in mine and looked into her eyes. "Your father has a broken leg."

"Oh no." I put a hand over my eyes. "If my father loses his leg…"

"No," he said. "It's broken. It will heal."

"I hope you're right," I said, searching his eyes. "That may be true in the future, but broken legs sometimes have to be taken off."

He turned a funny shade of green. "It will heal."

I nodded. I had to believe him. "What about the driver? Virgil?"

"I don't know. He saved your parents, but no one has seen him sense."

I shook my head. "I hope nothing happened to him."

"Keep your spirits up, my love," he said.

My face flushed at the unexpected endearment.

I had a vague memory of being trapped inside the carriage. I quickly put it away.

"You rescued me?"

"Yes," he said.

I looked into his blue eyes. Maybe I hadn't been dreaming after all. Maybe he'd really been here.

"I don't understand how you found me," I said.

He smiled a curious little grin. "Neither do I. I think it was fate."

I smiled back at him. Fate. Sometimes fate could be a wonderful thing.

35

JAMES

"I don't think I'm supposed to tell you anything about the future," I said.

I was sitting with Emma on a soft bear rug in front of the cabin's fireplace. I'd shoved the bed back some we were using it as a backrest.

She had rested for two days and we were going home in the morning. The snow and ice had melted after today temperatures that must have been at least in the forties.

"Why not?" she asked, looking up at me with that perplexed expression that she wore more often than not.

"I don't know," I said. "They say it could change the future."

"They," she said. "They always think they know more than they do."

I laughed out loud. "You're so right. I've always thought so, too."

"Then don't listen to them," she said, pulling a blanket around her shoulders.

"Are you cold?" I asked, helping her straighten it.

"A little," she said. "but I'm okay."

I couldn't help worrying that she was going to get sick and I wouldn't be able to help her. It had already been bad enough that she'd been close to hypothermia and I couldn't call for help.

"Can I check your toes?" I asked. I'd already asked her that about a dozen times.

"My toes are fine," she said.

I nodded.

"But okay."

"Really?"

"You may as well," she said, "but I don't know what you're going to do if I have frostbite."

I grinned at her. I'd spent some time explaining to her all about the dangers of frostbite. I wasn't a doctor or anything, so I probably added in some information that may or may not be accurate, but I'd wanted her to be safe. I didn't want her to lose any toes.

"I don't either," I said.

She shot me a glance.

I pulled her feet out from beneath the blanket and examined her toes. Her feet were perfect. No signs of frostbite.

"You're good," I said, my voice a bit husky. I cleared my throat and sat back.

"Are you sure?" she asked. "Because I don't want to lose any toes."

"Give me that," I said, pulling one of her feet into my lap and starting to massage her feet.

She leaned her head back and closed her eyes.

Someone knocked on the door.

"Who's that?" she asked, looking at me with alarm.

"I don't know."

But I did know that the door didn't have a lock on it. So whoever it was, I had no defense against them.

There was an iron poker in front of the fireplace, so I slowly reached over and wrapped my fingers around it.

I met Emma's wide-eyed gaze.

"Who is it?" I asked.

36

EMMA

I'd slept more in the last three days than I had ever slept in my life. And I'd been colder than I'd ever been. The old cabin was drafty. And there weren't a lot of ways to stay warm other than being under this blanket and sitting in front of the fire.

James had stayed right with me, tending to my every need. And he'd been a perfect gentleman.

The day had been warmer, but still too cold to move about much. And James had insisted that I continue to rest.

Tomorrow. He said we'd go home tomorrow.

I was ready to go home, but I was not ready to leave him. I didn't know what would happen when we got home.

Would he go away again? Or would he stay?

I'd thought we were alone, but someone was here, at the door of the abandoned cabin. Perhaps it was the owner. We'd have to explain why we were here.

"Who is it?" James called out.

"It's me. Virgil."

"Virgil," James said. "Isn't that your driver?"

"Yes," I said, sitting up and pulling the blanket tighter around me.

Virgil had rescued Father and Mother, then none of us had seen him again.

James got up and opened the door.

"Are you alright?" he asked.

Virgil nodded. "Did you find Emma?"

"Yes. She's here. She's well."

"Thank God," Virgil said.

"Do you want to come in?"

"Oh no, Sir," Virgil said. "I'll make camp over yonder."

"Nonsense," James said, stepping back and holding the door wide. "We have plenty of warmth in here."

"It ain't fitting."

"Come on, we're letting the heat out."

Virgil, however reluctantly stepped inside.

"Miss," he said to me.

"Hello Virgil," I said. "Where did you go? We were worried."

"I saw Mr. and Mrs. Becquerel heading the White's house and I followed them. I was hoping to get help. For you. But they said Mr. James would find you. That I should come with them."

"I tried to fight them. Said you needed me, but Mr. Becquerel insisted."

"It's okay, Virgil," I said.

I didn't understand why my father hadn't sent Virgil back to help James rescue me from the river, but all in all, it had worked out well. I'd gotten to spend time alone with James.

Spending time alone with a man was scandalous under normal circumstances, but in this situation, it would be excused.

Now that little interlude was over. Because now we had a chaperone.

Virgil took a seat across the room at the little roughhewn dining room table while James sat next to me on the floor.

"I guess we should get some sleep," he said. "so we can be rested in the morning."

I curled up and put my head on the pillow while James added wood to the fire.

And as I drifted to sleep I realized that he had managed to avoid telling me anything about the future, after all.

37

JAMES

The next day was warm and sunny.

I insisted that Emma ride Skye Traveler while I walked alongside them. Virgil walked a few yards ahead.

"We can both ride the horse," Emma said.

"I don't want to risk it."

"Risk what?"

"I'm not that good of a rider."

That was only part of the truth. The other part was that I didn't trust myself to be that close to her and to still keep my hands to myself.

One of the first things she'd told me was that she didn't like handsy men. I didn't plan on inadvertently falling into that category.

"What will you do?" she asked. "when we get back?"

"I'm not sure."

That was actually a very good question. And even though I badly needed an answer to it, I didn't have one.

I was good at running businesses. That was about it. I had an MBA in business management. I couldn't see how that could possibly be useful here in 1858. Here I would need to know how to be a farmer. Or maybe a carpenter.

"What did you do in your time?" she asked.

"I managed our family's business."

She didn't say anything as we continued our way toward her home.

"I guess you need a business to manage," she said.

"I guess I do. But I have a feeling that isn't something that there's a lot of around here."

"My father has a business," she said.

"I don't know anything about farming."

"What do you know?"

I shifted the horse's reins from hand to the other and back again. Watched a flock of birds flying south. Wasn't they a bit late.

"James?"

"Sorry. I know how to motivate people into getting work done. I know how to hire people and fire them."

"You're right," she said. "There aren't very many jobs around here for you."

"If I stay in this time," I said. "I'll have to figure something out."

"How will you decide?" she asked. "About whether or no you're going to stay?"

How would I?

It all depended on her and she didn't even know it. I would stay here. I would choose to be here with her. But would her father allow it?

"Do you think your father would allow me to court you?" I asked, looking over at her.

She looked back at me with her mesmerizing green eyes and grinned.

"Why wouldn't he?"

"Because in his eyes, I'm little more than a drifter. A man with no prospects."

Emma seemed to consider. She straightened the skirts of what had no doubt once been a lovely crimson dress.

"I don't know," she said. "I think he might see you as the man who saved my life."

"Maybe," I said. But it seemed that would be a bit too easy.

But was this the answer?

Was this how I managed to get back on my feet? I would have to go into town. Find a job. Build my reputation and my money.

Then. And only then would I feel worthy of courting Miss Emma Becquerel.

38

EMMA

It was odd being at home without my parents. It was almost like living alone. With the staff, of course, but still alone.

James had dropped me off, then had busied himself with working on things around the house.

He'd chopped a lot of firewood and done some work in the flower garden. After the big freeze, there were a lot of plants that needed pruning and such.

I busied myself with taking care of household things like meal planning and making sure the staff knew what to do around the house.

Running a household was a whole lot more work than it looked like from the outside. My mother made it all look so easy.

I didn't know where James slept. In fact, the only time I saw him was when I caught a glimpse of him outside.

I suppose he found his own way to the kitchen and ate there.

Today I decided it was time to get things back in order.

"Villars," I said, as I arranged some fresh flowers in a vase in the foyer. I'd cut them myself, even though I knew my mother didn't like flowers to be cut.

Well, she wasn't here and I liked fresh-cut flowers. Besides, I'd hoped I would run into James outside in the garden.

But I hadn't.

"Yes ma'am," Villars said. "What can I help you with Miss Emma?"

"Would you find Mr. James and invite him in to supper tonight?"

"Yes ma'am. If he asks, what's the occasion?"

"There isn't one," I said. "But if he asks, you can tell him it's for saving my life."

"Yes ma'am," Villars said.

Though he didn't say, I was quite sure that all the staff had heard about the carriage accident. Virgil would have told them.

"Please let me know what he says," I said as Villars walked off.

I spent the next thirty minutes wandering the house, finally ending up in the library.

But I didn't read. Instead I went to my father's desk and sat down in his chair.

I needed to talk to my cousin Nathan. I'd been puzzling over what Nathan had told me since that day we'd return from the little cabin.

Deciding there was no time like the present, I pulled a shawl over my shoulders and set off toward Nathan and Sophia's house. It was about a twenty-minute walk from here down a path toward the river.

The mournful wail of a steamboat horn spilled through the air and as I neared Nathan and Sophia's house, I heard the sound of children laughing.

Sophia sat on the front balcony, a sketch pad in her lap while her two children played in the yard in full view.

With a third baby on the way, Sophia was glowing.

Motherhood suited her. She'd told me once that she never really saw herself married with a family.

When she saw me, she waved and motioned for me to come up and sit with her.

"How are you?" she asked. "I heard about your accident. And I was meaning to come visit, but…" she motioned from her stomach to the two babies playing on the lawn.

"It's okay," I said. "And I'm okay."

"And your parents?" She was sketching something. I peeked over to see what she was doing. As usual, she was sketching a house plan. Most women relaxed by doing needlepoint, but not Sophia. Sophia relaxed by creating house plans.

"At the White's house. I haven't heard anything else, so I guess they're okay other than Father's broken leg."

"It sounds like it was a horrible experience," she said. "And you were lucky that guy showed up when he did."

"James," I said. "His name is James."

"Where is James from?"

I looked at her, trying to decide how much to tell her.

"Atlanta," I think. "But… he's also where you're from."

"Where's that?" she asked, her fingers still as she looked over at me.

"From the future."

39

JAMES

I hadn't been avoiding Emma. At least not exactly. I'd been trying to make myself useful while trying to decide what I was going to do.

I figured if I built up enough credit by helping out, I could borrow a horse and go into town to look for a job.

Since these were the days before commuting, I didn't know what I was going to do about a living situation. If it wasn't too far, I could travel back and forth. That option, however, was a last resort.

I'd never been one of those people who were content to commute to work an hour one way and then back home again.

I'd always lived near where I worked. It seemed to make life so much easier.

When Villars came with the message inviting me to dinner, I knew that I had stayed away from Emma for too long.

Her parents weren't home, so I didn't want to be improper by calling on her without a chaperone present. It was not a good idea to get off on a bad foot.

But, of course, I agreed that it was time for us to see each other again. I hadn't seen her since dropping her off after we'd gotten back.

I was wearing the only clothes I had—a pair of jeans and a sweatshirt. Hardly appropriate clothing to wear to dinner.

"You'll be needing something to wear," Villars said. "And a bath."

It was hard to build up credit when I kept using it about as fast as I could earn it.

"That would be great," I said. "Thank you."

"Meet me in the kitchen in an hour," Villars said. "I'll have everything ready."

"I can help with the water," I said.

"You're a guest here, Mr. James," Villars said. "I can't let you do that."

It was not a good idea to argue with the butler. But I didn't want to be a guest here. I want to live here. To be a part of the family.

And I'd been avoiding the one person who would make me part of the family. The person who made me want to be part of the family.

So I finished chopping the stack of firewood I was working on and headed toward the kitchen.

I looked for Emma as I passed the veranda, hoping to spot her sitting on a chair or the swing, but she was never outside. I listened for piano music, but she never played anymore.

If she hadn't invited me to dinner, I would have thought that she was avoiding me. Or that she wasn't even here.

But I was the man and I was supposed to do the courting.

So that's what I would do, I decided.

I would stop avoiding her.

If she didn't understand that I was currently out of work, then I would move to the next step. Whatever that was.

I went in through the west kitchen door into what was

known as the bathing room. It was really no more than an area partitioned off next to one of two fireplaces with a big porcelain bathtub filled with steaming hot water.

40

EMMA

I'd stayed with Sophia for at least an hour, maybe more. She'd explained to me that by inviting James to dinner, I had essentially asked him on a date.

She explained how people in the future dated.

I decided that I needed to put in some extra effort to get ready. I had a pretty silver dress I could wear. It wasn't as pretty as my crimson dress that had been damaged beyond repair had been, but it was still a lovely dress.

Relaxing in the steaming hot tub of hot water filled with magnolia scented bubbles, I ducked my head beneath the water and sat up, wiping the soap from my eyes.

I reached toward the wooden stool for a wash cloth, but a wash cloth appeared in my hand.

What?

Squinting, I peeked over the side of the tub.

James stood there, grinning at me.

I gasped and ducked back down.

"It seems we both had the same idea," he said.

"What are you doing here?"

"Villars said to meet him here for a bath."

I clutched the side of the tub, pulling bubbles over me.

"Villars never messes up like this," I said. "He must be getting up in age."

"In all fairness," he said, having backed away toward the door now. "I was a little early."

"A little… early…" I muttered to myself.

I peeked over the tub again. James was still fully dressed.

Thank God. If he'd undressed without seeing me, then… I…

I ducked back down, the water up to my chin.

The thought actually wasn't so bad.

The image of him here in the tub with me.

"You should go," I said, before the thought took hold and got me into trouble.

When he didn't answer, I peeked over again. He was already gone.

I sighed.

James was trouble.

And if I wasn't careful, he was going to get me into trouble.

It was time for me to get out, so I had time for my hair to dry before tonight.

So much for my nice relaxing bath. My heart was pounding like a racehorse.

James must think me forward indeed.

First, I'd asked him dinner and second, I'd been in the bathing room at the same time he was. I hope he didn't think I had orchestrated this.

The very thought had me blushing from head to toe.

I grabbed the big towel and wrapped it around me as I stood up.

I would just have to make sure that I was extra ladylike and demure so he didn't think me one of those forward women.

I didn't care that Sophia insisted that women in the future—James's time period—courted in an equal fashion. We were in my time, so we needed to follow the rules of my time.

41

JAMES

Holy hell.

I'd come about one inch from shedding my clothes and jumping into the steaming hot tub of water.

Fortunately, I'd heard a splash first.

Wasn't Emma supposed to have a lady's maid with her when she took a bath?

What was she doing all alone in there? There were three other people on the other side of the partition. A cook and two other people. One of them was a teenage boy.

For a culture to be so intent on propriety, they were certainly lax about the bathing room.

Not that I would have minded sharing a bath with Emma.

But that was surely not what Villars had in mind.

By the time I composed myself, Villars was walking along the path toward me.

"You're early," he said.

"You have no idea," I said, mostly to myself.

"Are you ready for your bath?" Villars asked.

I shook my head. "We can't go in there right now."

"Why not?" Villars asked. "I had the water boys fill a tub for you."

"It's occupied," I said.

"By whom?" Villars put his hands on his hips.

"Emma," I said.

Villars turned about as pale as a man of his dark coloring could.

"I see," he said.

"We should move away from the door," Villars said after about a minute of silence with neither of us saying anything.

"Of course."

Feeling like a naughty school boy, I followed Villars around to the other door on the east side, the one on the side of the kitchen.

"You can wait here, Sir," Villars said. "I must return to the house."

"Of course."

And he just left me here to sit at the work table with a cook shooting me displeased glances.

As a guest, I wasn't supposed to be in the kitchen.

It was past time I moved past the whole being a guest phase. It looked like I wasn't going anywhere.

So they might as well accept that I was here to stay.

At least that's what I told myself.

I was here to stay.

Unless, of course, I'd frightened Emma into asking me to leave. I needed to know what she was thinking.

And her parents weren't even home.

So I had to be extra sensitive to propriety.

42

EMMA

My hands shook as I tied the bow at the back of my waist.

Most girls had a lady's maid. I'd had a nanny when I was younger, but she had retired and since then I'd been on my own.

I suppose in times like this it would have come in handy to have someone to help with my bath and to help get dressed, especially since my hands didn't seem to want to work right now.

I'd invited James to eat dinner with me. Not to bathe with me.

Mon Dieu.

The most disturbing thing was I rather liked the idea.

My thoughts were scandalous.

In fact, I really didn't know where they came from.

Ever since James had kissed me, I had been replaying it over and over in my mind. And then when we'd been in the cabin, I'd been asleep most of the time, but he'd been such a gentleman, he hadn't even come close to kissing me.

I still had not quite sorted out how I came to be out of my crimson dress.

I hadn't asked and he hadn't said.

He'd been such a perfect gentleman.

But the way he'd grinned at me when he'd seen me peeking over the side of the tub, maybe not so much.

Finally getting my dress tied, I tugged on my boots and laced them up. Same problem. Shaky hands.

Leaving everything for the water boys to take care of, I slipped out the side door. I halfway expected and maybe even hoped a little bit that James would be there waiting for me.

But there was no one.

So I walked along the path toward the house. The sun was warm on my skin, but I shivered from having wet hair.

If I had a lady's maid, I could have her run hot tongs over my hair to dry it more quickly. Ah well. Such newfangled things were probably overrated.

I'd just let it dry naturally like I always did.

I would however, wrap a blanket around me and sit in front of the fireplace.

Going in the back door of the house, I met Villars.

"Miss Emma," he said, not looking at me directly.

"Villars," I said. "Is everything alright?"

"Everything is quite alright, Miss." He kept walking.

I shrugged and did the same.

There was a warm fire in the parlor and since it had the warm evening sun, what there was of it, that's where I would sit to dry my hair.

As I walked past the grandfather clock, it began to chime three times. Three o'clock. Just three more hours before my *date* with James.

Mon Dieu.

I was nervous as a schoolgirl.

43

JAMES

I whistled as I walked through the gardens toward the back door.

I felt more like a normal human being than I had in days. Bathed and wearing clean clothes. Even if they were old-fashioned clothes.

As I passed the roses, pinks, red, and whites, I wondered if I should take her a flower. But it just seemed wrong to take a girl a flower cut out of her own flower garden.

I slowed as I reached the steps leading up to the back veranda.

This didn't seem right.

I was courting her. I was not the help.

So I changed course and went around to the front of the house.

I walked right up the front steps, across the veranda, and knocked on the door.

I guess I was expecting Emma to answer the door, since seeing Villars standing there startled me a bit.

"Come in Mr. James." Villars held the door open and I stepped inside.

It was warm in the house compared to outside. Outside the air was turning cold as the sun went down.

It was December, after all, even in Natchez.

"You can wait in the parlor," Villars said. "Miss Emma will be down shortly."

"Thank you."

Villars left me standing there and I went into the parlor. Again, I was struck by how I didn't like being treated as a guest.

In my time, in the future, I had my own room, albeit a guest room. And I was free to roam the house.

Here, however, I was limited to where I was allowed to go.

I walked over to the silent piano. Ran a finger along the smooth keys.

If I closed my eyes, I could almost hear Emma's fingers flying over the keys, missed notes and all.

"Hello," she said from behind me.

I whirled around. Emma stood in the doorway. She wore a full skirted silver gown with a low décolletage. Her brunette hair swirled around her shoulders.

When she smiled at me with those full kissable lips, my heart did flips.

"Hi," I said, at least I think I said it out loud.

"It's so nice of you to come," she said. "Would you like to sit?"

"You look beautiful," I said.

She went to a chair, sat gracefully, leaning forward, and motioned for me to sit across from her on the sofa.

Villars stood at the door. Apparently he was acting as chaperone in the absence of her parents. What he didn't know was that we were way beyond this stage.

I did as she suggested. It looked like it was going to take all my skill and charm to get her attention again.

Not knowing what had happened was the worst. If I didn't know what had happened, how could I fix it?

"Would you like something to drink?" she asked.

"A whiskey," I said.

Villars moved to the liquor cabinet, poured whiskey into a glass, and brought it to me.

"Thank you, Villars," I said.

This was going to be an interesting night. Not at all what I expected.

44

EMMA

I was being overly formal. I knew this, but it was merely to make sure James didn't think I was a woman of ill-repute.

I didn't want him to think I was one of those women to be found in Natchez Under the Hill. I'd heard my brother and my cousins talk about them enough to know that they were not the sort of women that men married.

"Are you going to have a drink?" he asked.

"No," I said, shaking my head. Didn't he know that ladies didn't drink liquor?

"Thank you for inviting me to dinner," James said, after taking a sip of whiskey.

"You're welcome," I said. "It was the least I could do after you saved my life in the river."

He took another sip of whiskey, then nodded in my direction. "You don't have to thank me."

"Of course I do," I said, dismissing his words with a wave of my hand. "It'll be a few minutes until dinner is ready."

"Might I make a request?" he asked.

"Of course," I said, hoping my voice was much calmer than

my skittering heartbeat. I was at a loss to resist any request he might have.

"Would you play the piano?"

My smile faltered.

Despite my mother's efforts at making me into a proficient pianist, I was not.

"I'm afraid I'm not good."

"I think you sell yourself short," he said with a lift of his eyebrow.

I wiped my hands on my skirt and shot a glance toward the piano.

"Surely you wouldn't have me embarrass myself," I said, shifting my gaze back to his. He was looking at me with those intense blue eyes that I could not resist.

"You could humor me," he said, with a little sideways grin that did funny things to my heart.

"Oh, very well," I said. "But you'll regret it, I can assure you."

"Never," he said.

I got up and with a flourish of my skirts, I moved over to the piano, pulled some sheet music out of the bench, and sat down on the bench.

As I set the music on the stand, I glanced over at him. "Don't say I didn't warn you."

"Duly noted," he said, grinning at me over the back of the sofa, his chin propped on his hands.

I rolled my eyes and focused on the music standing in front of me.

I took a deep breath and began to play.

My fingers flew over the keys, the happy music spilling over me, filling my soul with a lightness I hadn't expected.

I closed my eyes, putting everything around me out of my mind.

My fingers slid over the keys so easily I wasn't even sure it was me playing.

With a smile on my lips, I looked over at James.

My fingers faltered on the keys, sending a discordant melody through the air.

My gaze shifted to Villars. He stood there, one hand on his forehead.

When his gaze met mine, I knew.

James was gone.

45

JAMES

I sat on the sofa, my eyes closed.

I had a clear memory of her sitting at this piano ten years ago, not playing so well, but that was a long time ago.

Emma had obviously underestimated her ability to play the piano. Either that or she was overly modest. Maybe that's what young ladies in the 1800s did. Perhaps it was their way of being demur.

But it was nothing like she had led me to expect.

She played like an angel.

The grandfather clock chimed the hour, providing a background for the piano music.

As the clock chimed the seventh time, Emma stopped playing as well.

Both the clock and her music lingered in the air.

As I raised my glass to her in a toast, I opened my eyes.

And blinked.

Emma was not sitting at the piano. She had vanished.

I whirled around, searching for her, but as I did, my gaze swept the room.

I was in a different room. Or rather I should say the same room in a different time.

The parlor was empty. I immediately recognized the electric lamps. And the television.

The television was the most obvious dead giveaway.

Emma had not vanished.

I had.

I was back in the future. In my own time.

This was not supposed to happen.

I was supposed to be with Emma.

I stood up and paced to the foyer. Looked into the quiet face of the grandfather clock with the rip between the six and the seven.

The broken clock.

The last I remembered here was Jonathan and Ophelia sitting together in the parlor. Laughing. Enjoying getting reacquainted after… what? Fifty years or so.

Was fate playing some kind of cruel trick on me. Jonathan was reunited with his high school sweetheart while I was ripped away from the arms of the woman I loved.

I walked over to the piano and sat down on the bench and ran my fingers over the smooth keys.

I felt nothing of Emma here. No scent. No lingering sound. Nothing.

In a moment of reckless anger, I jabbed a finger against one of the keys. It sounded hollow and meaningless.

I swirled around on the bench and covered my head with my hands.

Had I merely gone back in time to save Emma's life?

Was that it? Was that my sole purpose in going back?

I'd been led to believe that the time travel reunited soul mates.

I thought… I had… found my soul mate in Emma.

Yet the fates of time refused to allow us to be together.

I had decided that I wanted to live in the past. With Emma.
Yet here I sat. In the twenty-first century.
Why?
I needed to talk to Jonathan.
He was the only one with answers.

46

EMMA

It was a busy day in the Becquerel home.

Today my parents were coming home.

Though my father still couldn't walk on his broken leg, he had imposed too much on the White's hospitality. He had sent for Virgil and a wagon yesterday and a return message had arrived this morning that Virgil would be bringing him and Mother home today.

All of us, me and the staff, were frantically working to get everything ready for them. The house had to be cleaned. A bedroom set up downstairs since Father couldn't do the stairs.

And everything had to be put back like they had left it.

I tossed out all the fresh flowers so that Mother wouldn't know I'd cut them, washed the vases, and set them back out empty.

Two days had passed since James had vanished into what I believed had to be the future. His own time.

Sophia and Mackenzie had taught me more about the future than James had. James had kept what he knew close to the vest.

While straightening up, I ran across his computer in the library. I hadn't even given it to him.

I needed to put it somewhere. Somewhere my parents wouldn't see it. Even though they knew about the time travel, I didn't want to answer questions.

Carrying the computer, close against my chest, I took it with me through the foyer.

Just as I was about to go up the stairs, Sophia and Nathan appeared at the front door with their two children in tow.

I went to the door and opened it.

"We thought maybe you could use some help getting ready for the big return," Nathan said. "We know how picky Aunt Eloise can be."

"I think we've just about got it," I said. "But I am glad to see you. Both of you. Please come inside."

Outside, leaves were blowing on the cool wind. I was glad I didn't have to travel in this weather.

After what happened with the carriage, I wasn't sure I ever wanted to ride in a carriage again, much less in cold weather.

"What's that?" Sophia asked.

"James's computer," I said. "Mackenzie didn't tell you about it?"

"No," Sophia said. "I've haven't seen her."

"Can I see it?"

At my nod, Sophia thrust her daughter into Nathan's arms and we went into the parlor.

Sophia opened the computer.

"This is amazing," she said. "The batteries are lasting so much longer."

"And they're thinner," I added.

Sophia looked at me with an odd expression. "Yes," she said. "This belongs to James?"

I nodded.

"Where is he?" She looked around, as though expecting him to join us at any moment.

I shook my head.

"Gone again," she said.

"Yes." My eyes teared up. I'd been strong until now. But talking with someone about it made it worse somehow.

Sophia closed the computer and stared into space. I could almost see her thoughts whirling inside her head.

"Something's off," she said.

"What?" I asked, feeling hopeful for the first time in two days.

"I don't know for sure. But it's something." She tapped her fingers against her baby bump that was getting bigger by the day.

"Do you want him to come back?" she asked.

"Of course."

"How much?" she asked. "Are you sure he's the one for you?"

"Yes." I didn't know how to be much more sure. "I think about him all the time."

"Does he feel the same way?" she asked.

"I don't… I don't really know."

"That's it then," Sophia said. "You haven't solidified your bond."

"What?"

"Want to try something?" she asked.

"Okay."

Holding the closed computer carelessly under one arm, she grabbed my hand with the other and led me to the library.

She opened the bottom drawer and took out a piece of paper and some kind of writing pen.

Sitting in the chair, she wrote:

. . .

Dearest James,

Come back to my time. I miss you.

I'm waiting for you. I'll wait for you forever.

Love,

Emma

She slid it around for me to see.

"Is that how you feel?" she asked.

"Pretty much," I said. "but how are you going to get that to him?" I asked.

"I'm not sure we are," Sophia said. "But it's worth a try."

47

JAMES

I didn't sleep well at all, and was up the next morning before daylight.

It was clearly going to be one of those cold, dreary winter days.

As the coffee brewed, I went to the back door and found a newspaper leaning up next to the door.

Whoever delivered Jonathan's newspaper was an expert at it. Always on time and always next to the door.

I dropped it out of the plastic sleeve and laid it out on the table.

I heard Jonathan coming down the hallway before he made it to the door. Whistling.

"Good morning," he said when he saw me.

"Morning," I said. "Coffee?"

"Absolutely," he said, sitting down and reading the paper's headlines.

He didn't seem surprised to see me. I poured his coffee and stirred in some sweetener.

Made one for myself with some creamer then put them on the table.

"So how long was I gone?" I asked.

He looked up in surprise.

"You were gone?"

I sipped my coffee. Blew out a breath.

"How long?" he asked.

"I lost track."

"Well hell," Jonathan said, absently stirring his coffee.

"Why?" I asked. "Why does it keep happening?"

"I don't know," Jonathan said, sipping his coffee. "Do you want to be there? Or have you decided?"

"I do want to be there. I was prepared to stay this time."

We sat in silence a few minutes, sipping our coffee.

"How did it go with Ophelia?" I asked.

Jonathan smiled.

"Better than I ever would have imagined," he said. "Vaughn was the love of my life. But Ophelia is... pleasant to talk with."

I could see by the little smile playing about his lips that she was going to be good for him.

"Going to see her again?" I asked.

"She's coming back today."

"That's fast," I said.

Jonathan just shrugged. "We're not getting any younger."

I laughed. Truer words had never been spoken.

"Got anything to eat?" Jonathan asked.

"I can make you some toast," I said, not even bothering to tell him that this was his house.

As I waited for the toast to brown, I stared out the window. A flock of little brown birds landed on the ground outside and busied themselves with pecking the dirt for something to eat.

"After breakfast, we should check the mail," Jonathan said.

48

EMMA

The next two days passed quickly. Having my parents home again put everything in a whirlwind. It was a lot of work bringing their bed, clothes, and everything else they might possibly need downstairs. It could be months before Father could use the stairs again.

Since he was older, almost forty-years-old, there was no telling how long it would take him to heal. Could be months.

Since Mother was spending her time with him, the meal preparation fell on my shoulders. I went back and forth between the house and kitchen several times.

Each time, I had to bundle up in a heavy cloak and then warm up in front of the fireplace when I got inside. Perhaps one day kitchens would be part of the main house. Smaller houses were set up that way. I know having the kitchen outside was designed to help prevent fires, but it was so monumentally inconvenient.

I stood in front of the fireplace in the parlor after my seventh trip out to the kitchen in preparation for dinner.

And there were only going to be three of us. I shuddered to think what must go into hosting an actual dinner party.

Tomorrow I was going to do something different. I didn't know what it was yet, but it was going to be something, even if was wrong.

"There you are," Mother said, coming to stand next to me in front of the fire.

"Were you looking for me?" I asked.

"You look tired," she said, sweeping a strand of hair out of my face. "What have you been doing?"

"I've been getting everything ready for dinner tonight."

"Are we having guests?" she asked.

I shook my head and forced a little smile. "No, just the three of us." I paused. "Father?"

"Your father will take dinner in his room tonight. He's exhausted from the trip."

"I guess there will just be two of us then." And if given the choice, I was pretty sure I would have taken dinner in my room, if that were an option.

"I think I should have spent more time teaching you the fine art of running a home and less time trying to learn things like piano and needlepoint."

I smiled over at her and felt some of the tension drain away. Maybe running a home wasn't always this hard. Because if it was, I was wondering if maybe I needed to find myself a little cabin in the woods and forego living on an estate.

"I'm sure piano and needlepoint are important, too, Mother." No matter how hard Mother had been on me growing up, I couldn't bear the thought of her feeling bad for how she'd raised me.

She just shrugged. "Where is James?" she asked.

"I think he went back to his own time."

"I see," she said.

Silence hung in the air as Mother sat down and picked up her needlepoint from the basket beside her chair. I sat down, too, but just gazed absently into the flames.

"I've invited Edward White over for dinner tomorrow," Mother said. "I don't think you ever met him."

"Why?" I asked. "Why would you invite Edward White over here?" She and Father had just gotten home. Why was she inviting guest over already?

"I just think you should meet him," she said. "that's all. Besides, he'll be out here anyway, seeing some of his regular patients.

"I see," I said. I suppose Mother got to know the White family fairly well while she and Father were staying in their home.

"Emma," Mother said, setting her needlepoint in her lap and looking at me.

I drew my gaze from the fire and sat back in my chair to give her my attention.

She searched my eyes. "You don't know if James is coming back here or not."

Her words stabbed at something deep inside me. A thought… a reality that I didn't want to think about. To have her say it so matter of factly. Just like she would say *you don't know if it's going to rain today,* pierced my heart.

I lifted my chin and pulled my gaze from hers.

"I do know." I crossed my arms. Mother's words made me sick to my stomach. How could she say such a thing?

"And it doesn't matter. I'm going to wait for him. No matter how long it takes.

I gathered up my skirts and left my mother sitting there. As I hurried past the foyer, the grandfather clock began to chime the hour.

Just another reminder of how time stood between me and James.

I wasn't sure how I was going to survive that *however long it takes* I'd just proclaimed that I would wait for.

49

JAMES

I didn't say anything as I put butter on four slices of toast and put a jar of jelly on the table.

If Jonathan wanted to check the mailbox, then I guess we could walk down the oak lined dirt road and check it. Didn't seem like much point to it, since the mailman drove the mail up to the house every day and personally got out of his car to put the mail in the little wrought iron mailbox on the wall next to the door.

I poured orange juice into two glasses, then sat down at the table and slid one over to Jonathan.

"Thank you," he said.

It was unfortunate that Jonathan had found a companion late in life only to start showing signs of dementia.

We ate breakfast and read the paper in silence.

"Ready to check the mail?" Jonathan asked a few minutes later.

"Sure," I said. "Let me get my coat."

Jonathan stood up. "You won't need it. We're just going upstairs."

Upstairs. To check the mail.

Again, I worried that his mind was getting weak. Perhaps I'd take him in to the doctor. They had medicine to help with this sort of thing.

We left the kitchen, crossed through the foyer, and went upstairs.

I followed Jonathan straight to the guest room. Not the room I was using, but the other guest room.

He went to the closet and came back with a little pry bar and a small hammer.

"What's that for?" I asked.

Jonathan grinned. "It's how we check the mail." He pulled a stool over and sat in front of the window.

"Jonathan," I said, kneeling beside him. "I don't think—"

He wasn't paying me any attention, so I just watched as he carefully pried loose one side of the window frame.

Damned if a letter didn't fall out.

"What the—?"

Jonathan grinned as he tapped the window frame back in place.

"Sophia's invention," he said.

"Sophia."

"You didn't get a chance to meet her," he said. "Before she left."

"Where did she go?" I asked, watching him carefully as he picked up the letter and smoothed it out.

"She went back in time," he said, matter-of-factly. "This is probably for you." He handed the letter to me.

My hands shook as I carefully unfolded the letter and began to read.

Dearest James,

Come back to my time. I miss you.

I'm waiting for you. I'll wait for you forever.

Love,
Emma

I READ IT AGAIN. THEN DROPPED IT INTO MY LAP.

I looked over at Jonathan.

"What the hell?"

50

EMMA

I brushed my hair and pulled it up and back, leaving a loose strand to frame one side of my face.

I hadn't found a way to avoid dinner tonight. With such a small guest list—one—it would have been more than obvious.

Besides, it would have been the height of rudeness for me to not show up for any guest. Even Doctor Edward White—the man my mother wanted me to date.

I would be cordial, of course. I would be polite as befitting the daughter of a wealthy planter near Natchez, Mississippi.

At the sound of horse's hooves coming toward the house, I went over to the window to get my first glimpse of the mysterious Edward White.

He slipped off his horse and looped the reins over the hitching post. He was wearing a heavy cloak and hat with a scarf around his neck, so I couldn't get a sense of what he looked like.

I sincerely hoped Mother hadn't given him false hope about courting me.

I could not in good conscience allow him to court me when my heart belonged to another.

I turned away from the window before he saw me standing there and smoothed my skirts.

Might as well get this over with since I was dressed and coiffed, wearing a dress I'd only worn one time before. It was in a deep shade of green that reminded me of pine needles in the spring. It had a wide sash tied at the waist, with long ends left to flow along with the movement of the skirt.

The neckline was high and the sleeves were long. I draped a white wool shawl around my shoulders, making me feel rather elegant.

I left my room and headed downstairs.

The clock began to chime the hour as I reached the landing and Villars opened the door just as I started down the stairs.

He welcomed Edward inside and took his wraps. I got a good look at him without him seeing me first. He was a pleasant looking man and under other circumstances, I might have found him attractive.

I couldn't, however, keep from comparing him to James. Edward wasn't as tall and was leaner, skinny even. He was also painfully clean shaven making him looking far younger than James, though I knew he wasn't.

After Edward was ushered into the parlor, I went the rest of the way downstairs to join them.

Mother sat on the sofa next to Edward. He stood as I came to the door.

"There she is," Mother said, as I walked into the parlor to join them. "Emma, this is Doctor White."

"Please," he said, his brown eyes smiling into mine. "Call me Edward. Dr. White is my father."

When I put a gloved hand in his and he bent over my hand, I felt absolutely nothing.

"It's a pleasure to finally meet you," he said.

"Likewise." I walked over to the nearest armchair and sat

down, taking the time to arrange my skirts as I arranged my thoughts.

Edward could be a friend. He seemed pleasant enough and it never hurt to have a physician as a friend.

Villars came to the door.

"Dinner will be delayed," he said. "There was an incident in the kitchen."

"What kind of incident?" Mother asked. "Is anyone injured?

"No. No," Villars said. "Nothing like that. Just one of the dishes didn't turn out as expected and Cook had to start over."

"Oh, well," Mother said. "No harm. No foul."

"I brought some refreshments," he said. "to tide you over."

"That's very thoughtful," Mother said.

Villars turned and wheeled in a little cart filled with grapes and cheese and some crackers all very well presented on a platter.

"May I pour you all a glass of wine?" he asked.

Mother nodded and Villars went to the liquor cabinet, returning with three glasses of bubbly wine.

Mother lifted a brow as I took a glass from him, but she didn't say anything. I suppose she decided if I was old enough to have suitors, I was old enough to have a glass of wine.

"This is nice," Mother said. "Now all we need is some music."

Oh no. I could see it coming a mile away. Mother was about to put me out there, knowing how much I hated that.

"Emma," she said. "Why don't you play one of your songs for us?"

"Of course," I said, with a tight smile.

Taking my untouched glass of wine over to the piano, I sat down at the bench.

I swirled the wine in my glass, as I contemplated which song I would play, then took a sip. This was what exactly what

Mother had prepped me for. To impress suitors and other guests.

Well, I thought. She would get what she got. It was all I could do.

I put my hands on the keys and began to play.

The light melody came easy to me, but it didn't suit my mood, so I transitioned into something more melancholy. It was a song I'd heard my cousin Mackenzie play and I had spent some time learning it while I had the house to myself.

Oddly enough, I found that my fingers slid more easily over the tune than they did over the brighter, more light-hearted melodies.

It did, however, take more concentration to play by memory, so I put everything else out of my mind and focused on the movement of my fingers over the keys.

51

JAMES

For three days, I'd had the Weather Channel playing on every television in the house. There were four of them, all total, not counting the one in Jonathan's room. And I was pretty sure he had that one turned on as well.

There was nothing I could do, but if wishful thinking had anything to do with it, then I would going back in time at any moment.

Jonathan insisted that the weather had something to do with the time travel.

I needed a storm.

In the meantime, I went deep into the Internet and read everything I could about the nineteenth century.

For three days I immersed myself into the past. When—not if—I went back, I would know information about would then be history and as well as what would be the future. I didn't harbor any delusions that I could change the future. Not in any way. But I wanted to be prepared for whatever might come my way. I would have Emma to take care of. Emma and our children.

Taking a break from my computer, I sat outside on the back veranda with a glass of untouched whiskey.

Jonathan and Ophelia were inside They'd turned off the Weather Channel and were watching a movie. They were so cute together. Jonathan had grieved for Vaughn long enough. It was far time he enjoyed the company of a woman again.

I swirled my whiskey and allowed my thoughts to wander. They naturally went down their familiar path. To Emma.

I had a theory.

I believed that the reason I had lost everything was so that I could come here to Jonathan's. I'd been brought here for no explicable reason, really. And I had come here so I could go back in time to meet Emma.

So given all that, it made no sense to me why I would still be here and not back in the past.

Was I missing something? Or was it just not time yet?

I took a sip of the whiskey and felt its heat all the way down.

The wind rustled through the oak leaves, knocking more and more of them to the ground. The wind was bringing a storm with it.

The yard would need to be cleaned again soon, but my gut told me I wasn't the one who would be doing it.

My life waited for me in the past.

Emma had said she was waiting for me. Would wait for me forever. I felt the same about her.

And if I had Emma, then everything else would work itself out. I now had enough information in my head about how business worked in the 1800s. I was ready. We might not be wealthy right away, but I'd get us there.

I leaned back and closed my eyes.

That's when I heard the steady tick of the grandfather clock, followed by the chimes.

I counted them.

Eight chimes.

It was eight o'clock.

Then I heard music. Serious, almost melancholy music. No. I decided not melancholy.

Romantic. The music was romantic.

I sat there, my eyes closed and just listened.

Maybe Ophelia was playing the piano. It was a possibility, though I quickly dismissed it. She and Jonathan were deep into a movie, snuggled contentedly together.

After a few minutes, I realized I was listening for wrong notes.

But I didn't hear any.

If Emma was playing, she had gotten better. Much better.

I took a sip of the whiskey I held in my hand and smiled at myself.

Sophia had taken a Kindle back in time. And antibiotics. And special paper and pens. Jonathan had told me how hard she had worked getting everything prepared.

But out of all the things I could have brought back in time, I'd brought one of Jonathan's glasses with whisky.

I tipped it up and drained it. Then I went inside, taking the empty glass with me.

I dropped it off in the dining room—what had been the kitchen a few minutes ago. It no longer smelled like the popcorn Jonathan and Ophelia had popped. It just smelled like furniture wax mixed with what smelled a little like apple pie.

The music got louder as I neared the parlor.

Walking past the grandfather clock, I noted that it was in perfect condition. No scar across the face. And it was ticking as it should be.

I stopped at the parlor door and leaned against it.

There were three people in the foyer.

There was a young man I didn't recognize. A woman who had to be Emma's mother.

And then there was Emma.

She had her eyes closed. Much as she had the last time I'd seen her sitting at this piano.

Only this time, instead of a flirty expression, she wore a serious expression and there was a sadness about her.

In the letter, she'd said she was waiting for me. It was quite possible I had given that sadness to her.

But the young man watching me seemed unconcerned about any of that.

I didn't blame him. Emma was stunningly beautiful.

A stray lock of hair fell across her face as she looked down, but she wasn't looking at any music. She knew this music by memory.

It was a song of her heart.

I don't know how I knew that. I just did.

She ended the song and then she opened her eyes and looked right at me.

She thought she imagined me.

I knew from that blank expression on her face.

But then her mother and the young man turned and looked at me, too.

That's when she knew that she hadn't imagined me.

Go big or go home.

My father's words came back to me clear as a bell.

I walked across to the piano and stood in front of Emma.

As she looked into my eyes and blinked, I could see the moisture in her eyes. I held out a hand. She didn't hesitate to put her hand in mine.

Once she was standing, I looked at her mother, then the other fellow.

"My apologies for interrupting," I said. "But I need to borrow Emma for a few minutes."

Maybe more than a few minutes.

Maybe more like a lifetime, but we'd get to that later.

Since it was too cold to go outside, I led her to the library, grabbed a candle from one of the sconces, and closed the door behind us.

Once inside, she stepped into my arms and we just stood that way, holding each other as though we would never let go.

And if I had my way, I wouldn't.

She was first to loosen her hold. She leaned back enough to look into my eyes.

"Where have you been?" she asked with a little smile.

"I've been working my way back to you."

"Can you stay?" she asked.

"Yes," I said. After all, believing something was more than half the battle.

I put a palm on her cheek and kissed her.

This was where I belonged.

There was no question about that and there never would be again.

It had just taken a little time for us to get it all together.

Perhaps she had beckoned me with a song.

EPILOGUE

EMMA

One Year Later

I sat in the upstairs sitting room, watching the street below. I sat in a rocking chair, knitting a red stocking. It was the second one I had done and this one looked a lot better than the first one.

The city of Natchez was busy this time of year. Christmas time. Christmas was one week away and the city was bustling with activity.

James would be home soon. I could set a clock by his schedule.

We'd moved to Natchez last Spring. Two reasons. One, Sophia believed that the house was an integral part of a time portal. Her thinking was that if people moved away from the portal, they wouldn't go back through time again.

The other reason was that James needed an office in town. A place where people could come to him for meetings. A place easily accessible, unlike the estate.

Father had provided the initial investment, but James had already paid it back.

James obviously knew what he was doing and people liked him.

He was working with the bank doing some kind of investments. I didn't really understand it, but I didn't need to.

Then I saw James coming down the sidewalk, right on time. He opened the front gate of the white picket fence and closed it behind him.

Jumping up, I dropped the stocking into the chair and hurried downstairs. I reached the door and swung it open just as he reached it.

He grabbed me around the waist and twirled me around in a circle. Seeing him never got old.

He sat me on my feet and kissed me.

"I missed you," he said.

"You've only been gone four hours," I said, swatting playfully at his chest. I didn't tell him that I'd missed him, too, terribly so.

I have a surprise for you," he said.

"I have one for you, too," I said.

"You first," I said, though I was bursting at the seams with my own surprise.

He reached into his pocket and pulled out a little box.

"What is it?" I asked.

"Open it," he said, taking my hand and pulling me into the parlor.

We sat on the sofa and I opened the box.

"Is this my Christmas present?" I asked.

"It was supposed to be," he said, but I couldn't wait."

I opened it up and found a lovely ivory broach in the shape of music note.

"I feel like music brought us together somehow," he said.

"It's beautiful," I said, slipping into his arms. I pulled my feet up on the sofa and leaned against him.

"So what's your surprise?" he said, nuzzling me close.

I looked up at him and grinned.

"We're going to need to decorate the extra bedroom," I said, with an amazingly straight face.

"Why?" he asked. "Are we having guests?"

"Something like that," I said, running a hand down the little bump at my waist.

"Something like?" he asked, looking at me, obviously perplexed.

Men. So clueless. "We're going to have a baby."

"What?" He grabbed me up in his arms and kissed me on the mouth.

"We're going to have a baby!" he said.

"Are you happy?"

"Are you kidding me?" he asked, grinning from ear to ear. "This is the best news you could ever give me. I've gone from having absolutely nothing to having more than any man could ask for."

I nestled against his chest.

A family. We were starting a family of our own.

And nothing had ever felt more right.

Keep Reading for a Preview of Second Chance Kisses…

SECOND CHANCE KISSES

PREVIEW

CHAPTER 1
MADISON WORTHINGTON

This was not happening.

Not in a hundred years.

I stared at the schedule on the computer screen in front me. The caller on the other end of the phone line forgotten.

The least of my problems.

I forgot to breathe. Or maybe I just couldn't get any air.

How many Kade Johnsons were there?

How many Kade Samuel Johnsons?

How many Kade Samuel Johnsons who were pilots?

"Hello?"

Right. I was scheduling a flight for Markus Peters. One of Skye Travel's best customers.

Shit.

"I'm so sorry Mr. Peters. There was a glitch in the phone line." There was actually a glitch in my brain.

It had been eight years since I'd seen Kade Johnson.

Eight years.

And not a day in those eight years had passed that I hadn't had at least a fleeting thought of Kade Johnson in one way or another.

I put Mr. Peters on speaker and keyed in his information. He now had a flight to Florida with his family scheduled for Friday.

With Kade Johnson in the pilot's seat.

My little brother, Quinn, was going to hear about this. Had Quinn lost his mind?

"Thank you, Mr. Peters, for flying Skye Travels. We'll see you Friday."

I clicked off the phone and looked toward the conference room.

Fortunately for Quinn, he was tied up in a meeting for the next... I glanced at my watch... hour or so.

And by then, I'd be heading out.

It was only my first day on the job—sort of, but I'd been doing this work on and off, since I was a senior in high school.

A questionable perk of being the boss's daughter.

My father, Noah Worthington, believed his children should work like everyone else.

He didn't want us growing up soft, living off his money. And all five of his children had careers.

The only questionable one, though, was my little brother Quinn.

He'd gotten his business degree, then somehow slid right into the company as vice-president.

He claimed to be following in our father's footsteps, but I seemed to be the only one who noticed that Quinn had never flown an airplane.

Our father, however, was a well-known and respected pilot

and had formed his company, Skye Travels, based on that reputation.

I could see the tarmac from here. Close enough that the office carried the comforting scent of jet fuel. But right now even that wasn't enough to calm my nerves.

I had to get through the next hour. Then I could figure out what to do about this Kade Johnson thing.

I straightened up what was going to be my workspace for the next three months and checked my phone messages.

I had one text from my best friend Emily.

EMILY: *Are you off yet?*

ME: *Not yet. One hour left.*

EMILY: *Drinks at the Skyhouse?*

She completely read my mind. I'd only been back in town a few days and hadn't seen my best friend yet.

ME: *OMG. Yes.*

EMILY: *See you there.*

My fingers hovered over the keys. But I set my phone down. I wasn't ready to tell her about Kade. I was still processing it myself and I didn't need Emily's opinion tossed into my brain just yet.

Quinn stuck his head out of the conference room across the hall.

"Madison? Would you make some copies for us?"

"Of course." I put a big fake smile on my face for the benefit of the two men who were meeting with Quinn as I took the envelope from him.

The men were from a big marketing firm and Quinn was meeting them to set up a contract. I had to give Quinn credit. He was good at schmoozing.

But seriously. Quinn was taking advantage of me.

I should have a nameplate made for the receptionist desk.

Dr. Madison Worthington.

I squared my shoulders. I'd done it to myself. I was the one who'd volunteered to help out until he could hire someone for the summer. And then I'd be the one to train the new person.

The receptionist they'd had for years had retired last week. I had trained her myself during the summer before I left for graduate school. I seriously think she waited until she knew I was coming in for the summer before she announced it.

I didn't blame her. This way I was the one doing the training.

My father's work ethic was firmly cemented in my psyche.

I didn't begrudge it. That work ethic was what had gotten me through undergrad in three years. Then graduate school.

After getting my license to practice psychology, I'd done some teaching at Houston Community College and discovered that I liked it. Okay. Loved it.

At first, I couldn't believe they were paying me to do something that was so much fun.

It hadn't taken me long to land a full-time teaching job.

In Denver.

I had three months before I had to show up for new faculty orientation.

Since I already had my apartment secured, I had some time on my hands.

The copy room was at the other end of the office suite. Past the elevator.

Just as I stepped past the elevator, it dinged.

Skye Travels was known for not only its efficiency, but also its Houston hospitality.

I turned, holding the brown envelope Quinn had handed me against my chest and prepared to greet whoever stepped off the elevator.

But also, Quinn was waiting.

I took a step backwards.

The elevator doors opened.

And I froze.

Kade Samuel Johnson stepped off the elevator.

I was having that breathing problem again.

Maybe I should see a doctor about that.

But I already knew it was full-fledged anxiety.

And I knew how to treat it. I was a psychologist after all.

Take a deep breath.

Kade stepped out of the elevator. Stopped and looked right at me.

It was almost like he'd known I was standing there.

He wouldn't have known, of course.

Couldn't have known.

He looked at me blankly.

He didn't even recognize me.

We'd been together for three years and he didn't even recognize me.

I clamped down every thought that came to my head.

Kade worked here now.

My stupid, inconsiderate, clueless brother had hired him.

So I just turned around.

I turned around and continued to the copy room.

I wasn't about to let Kade Johnson know that I'd thought about him every day when he couldn't even have the decency to recognize me.

Sure. It had been eight years.

Sure. Instead of actually breaking up, we'd drifted apart.

But still.

I stepped into the copy room and opened the envelope.

My hands were shaking too much for me to do the simple task of pulling the papers out of the envelope and my eyes wouldn't focus.

Damn it.

This was not going to get the best of me.

I yelped as the envelope sliced across my right index finger giving me a paper cut.

I dropped the envelope onto the copier and stuck my bleeding finger in my mouth.

When I'd gotten up this morning, I'd had no idea that this would be the day I'd see Kade Johnson again.

And all the psychological training in the world was useless.

CHAPTER 2
KADE JOHNSON

I RECOGNIZED MADISON IMMEDIATELY, OF COURSE.

But I swear my body knew she was there before I did.

As soon as the elevator dinged and the door opened, it knew.

I'd always liked the scent of jet fuel, but it had never been a turn on.

Not like that.

It was definitely Madison.

By the time my brain caught up, she'd turned around and walked away.

My first instinct was to follow her. And I even took two steps forward before my logical brain reminded me that my instinct was eight years out of date.

She'd always been pretty. With a quick smile.

But the Madison who'd just walked away from me was not pretty. She was drop dead gorgeous.

Long, brunette mermaid hair. That perfect heart-shaped face. Lips that naturally turned up at the corners.

And a tight black skirt that did everything to remind me what I knew about that body beneath it.

She was wearing a white button-down shirt tucked into that skirt, revealing her narrow waist.

I bet I could still wrap my hands around that waist.

But I worked here now. And she was the boss's daughter.

I had to keep it together.

And keep it in my pants.

I needed a minute before I walked down to reception to meet up with Quinn.

The last thing I needed was to walk into my new office with a hard-on.

I'd only met Quinn Worthington once and during the interview calls, neither one of us had mentioned my previous relationship with his sister. It was possible he didn't even remember me from back then.

Not likely. But certainly possible.

He was younger than I was. Five years? Maybe more.

And when I'd been with Madison, Quinn had been away at a boarding school or some such to prep him for college.

It occurred to me then that Quinn might have hired me without telling Madison.

And if Madison worked here…

I thought she'd be far away from here by now.

I'd seen enough social media updates—not stalking—to know that she'd finished her degree in psychology.

She'd finished it just like she'd set out to do.

Madison completed everything she set out to do. It was one of the many things I admired about her.

Unfortunately, though, it had been the end of our relationship.

We'd decided not to do the whole long distance thing.

I don't know what she'd been thinking, but I always sort of thought we were on a break.

I'd dated, of course. It had been eight years after all and a man had needs.

But I'd never let myself get serious with anyone.

Was it because of Madison?

Not that I would ever admit it.

I turned left and went toward what looked like a lobby. All my interviews and discussions had been via facetime. My reputation was good enough to get me a job anywhere in the industry.

But life happened and I needed to be closer to home.

There was no one at the receptionist's desk. Quinn was in the glass-walled conference room on the other end of the lobby with two men.

I took a seat on one of the little sofas in the spacious lobby. This whole side of the office had floor to ceiling windows overlooking the tarmac.

I had an involuntary little sense of excitement. This third floor office space was perfect.

I should have known Noah Worthington would do it right. The man had gone from being a commercial pilot—like me—to owning a fleet of small jets. He had started out in Dallas/Fort Worth, but for some unknown reason, he'd moved his main office to Houston.

Rumors suggested it had something to do with his wife Savannah. And apparently they were living in Houston now.

The receptionist must have already left for the day. Not a problem. I didn't have anything else I had to do today.

I stretched out my legs and pulled out my iPad. Scrolled idly through my emails.

But. Damn it. I couldn't concentrate.

Madison was somewhere in this office. I know she recognized me, but she'd turned walked away.

At the sound of feminine heels coming toward me from the elevator area, I looked up.

And watched as Madison walked straight toward me.

I stood up. Bad idea.

Then she smiled and I nearly came undone.

CHAPTER 3
MADISON

KADE JOHNSON HAD GOTTEN EVEN MORE HANDSOME WITH AGE. But it was like that with guys.

He was wearing black slacks and a white button-down shirt. Basic pilot attire. Same basic outfit I was wearing except that I was wearing a skirt and heels, of course.

Was that why I had butterflies in my stomach? Just because we were wearing the same kind of clothes?

Of course not. Sometimes I put too much into all the psychological theories that had been hammered into my head.

He recognized me now. I could see it all over his face.

It had certainly taken him long enough.

I afforded him the same hospitality I'd give anyone visiting my father's company.

Only, he was doing more than just visiting. And since I was going to be working here for the next three months, I had no choice but to be cordial.

We'd parted as friends and promised to stay in touch.

That promise had been made eight years ago and I hadn't heard from him since that day we'd said good-bye in the parking lot of our favorite taco pub.

"Hello Kade," I said.

"Hello Madison." He smiled back.

I was impressed by how quickly he'd recovered from not recognizing me.

"You're working here now."

"What are you doing here?"

We both spoke at the same time.

We'd always had an uncanny kind of sync.

Was that how his first day and my first day were the same?

But no, I was being fanciful. I'd worked here on and off as needed over the years and this was the first time Kade had shown up.

It was just a weird quirk of chance.

Unless…

I narrowed my eyes in the direction of the conference room.

Had Quinn orchestrated this?

"Quinn didn't tell you, did he?" Kade asked, echoing my thoughts.

"No," I said. "But I saw your name on the schedule."

"Quinn moves fast," he said.

"We don't like to waste time here at Skye Travels." I held the envelope with the copies close to my chest. Like a shield.

"It's good to see you," he said. "But, seriously, what are you doing here?"

"Working," I said. "If you'll excuse me, I have to get these to Quinn."

I turned and walked straight for the conference door.

Quinn met me there and took the papers off my hands.

I went back to the reception desk, took my seat, and put the headset back on.

I did all this without glancing at Kade one single time.

I could do this.

I could be around him and not focus on him.

I was very pleased with my progress so far.

"Why aren't you somewhere straightening out lives?"

I jumped back, stifling a yelp.

Kade was leaning on the counter, smiling at me.

In my efforts to not look at him, I hadn't seen him move over to the reception desk.

Maybe this was going to be a bit harder than I thought.

Keep Reading Second Chance Kisses

Kathryn Kaleigh is the author of sixty-eight novels, over one hundred short stories, and many collections.

kathrynkaleigh.com

www.ingramcontent.com/pod-product-compliance
Lightning Source LLC
Chambersburg PA
CBHW030337310726
48979CB00001B/75
9781647913960